"I Want You. I Plan To Have You.

Donna glared at him. "I was right, Jake. You haven't changed a bit."

"Maybe you're right," he agreed softly. "But you're not a fifteen-year-old virgin anymore, are you?"

"No, I'm not," she said. "I'm an adult. A mother. With more to think about than feeding my own desires. Whatever's between you and me, it doesn't give you an opening to Eric."

He frowned at her and shook his head. "You don't get it, Donna. We don't *need* an opening to Eric. He's a Lonergan. That makes him one of us. Family."

"His name is Eric *Barrett*."

"Doesn't make him any less a Lonergan, or us any less his family."

Dear Reader,

Things are heating up in our family dynasty series, THE ELLIOTTS, with *Heiress Beware* by Charlene Sands. Seems the rich girl has gotten herself into a load of trouble and has ended up in the arms of a sexy Montana stranger. (Well...there are worse things that could happen.)

We've got miniseries galore this month, as well. There's the third book in Maureen Child's wonderful SUMMER OF SECRETS series, *Satisfying Lonergan's Honor,* in which the hero learns a startling fifteen-year-old secret. And our high-society continuity series, SECRET LIVES OF SOCIETY WIVES, features *The Soon-To-Be-Disinherited Wife* by Jennifer Greene. Also, Emilie Rose launches a brand-new trilogy about three socialites who use their trust funds to purchase bachelors at a charity auction. TRUST FUND AFFAIRS gets kicked off right with *Paying the Playboy's Price.*

June also brings us the second title in our RICH AND RECLUSIVE series, which focuses on wealthy, mysterious men. *Forced to the Altar,* Susan Crosby's tale of a woman at the mercy of a...yes...wealthy, mysterious man, will leave you breathless. And rounding out the month is Cindy Gerard's emotional tale of a pregnant heroine who finds a knight in shining armor with *A Convenient Proposition.*

So start your summer off right with all the delectable reads from Silhouette Desire.

Happy reading!

Melissa Jeglinski

Melissa Jeglinski
Senior Editor
Silhouette Books

Please address questions and book requests to:
Silhouette Reader Service
U.S.: 3010 Walden Ave., P.O. Box 1325, Buffalo, NY 14269
Canadian: P.O. Box 609, Fort Erie, Ont. L2A 5X3

MAUREEN CHILD

Satisfying Lonergan's Honor

Published by Silhouette Books
America's Publisher of Contemporary Romance

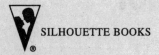 SILHOUETTE BOOKS

ISBN 0-373-76730-7

SATISFYING LONERGAN'S HONOR

Copyright © 2006 by Maureen Child

All rights reserved. Except for use in any review, the reproduction
or utilization of this work in whole or in part in any form by any
electronic, mechanical or other means, now known or hereafter
invented, including xerography, photocopying and recording, or in
any information storage or retrieval system, is forbidden without
the written permission of the editorial office, Silhouette Books,
233 Broadway, New York, NY 10279 U.S.A.

All characters in this book have no existence outside the imagination of
the author and have no relation whatsoever to anyone bearing the same
name or names. They are not even distantly inspired by any individual
known or unknown to the author, and all incidents are pure invention.

This edition published by arrangement with Harlequin Books S.A.

® and TM are trademarks of Harlequin Books S.A., used under license.
Trademarks indicated with ® are registered in the United States Patent
and Trademark Office, the Canadian Trade Marks Office and in other
countries.

Visit Silhouette Books at www.eHarlequin.com

Printed in U.S.A.

MAUREEN CHILD

is a California native who loves to travel. Every chance they get, she and her husband are taking off on another research trip. The author of more than sixty books, Maureen loves a happy ending and still swears that she has the best job in the world. She lives in Southern California with her husband, two children and a golden retriever with delusions of grandeur.

To my wonderful daughter Sarah
and her terrific new husband, Dan—
I wish for you the joy and love you both deserve

One

Jake Lonergan wasn't used to having so many people around. For fifteen years, he'd been a loner. Moving from one place to the next, one motorcycle race to the other. He didn't make friends and he didn't contact his family.

Made life simple.

And he probably would have gone on as he was for the next fifteen years if he hadn't gotten word his grandfather, Jeremiah Lonergan, was dying. The old man Jake loved had made only one request: that his three grandsons come home for one last summer together.

Jake had been in Spain when he got word, and

it had taken him long enough to get back to Coleville, California, that he'd been afraid Jeremiah would already be dead and buried. That he'd miss his chance to say goodbye.

It wasn't until he arrived that he'd discovered Jeremiah wasn't dying—he was just sneaky. The old man had tricked Jake and his cousins, Sam and Cooper, into coming home to the ranch they'd all avoided for fifteen years.

Jake gave the bolt on the undercarriage of his custom-built, black-and-chrome motorcycle one last turn, then stood up and stretched the kinks out of his back. He glanced out the double barn doors toward the ranch house across the yard. Lamplight pooled from every window and the low murmur of conversations and laughter floated to him on the otherwise still air.

Jake stared at the house for a long minute, feeling, as he always did, like the outsider. His own damn fault, of course. But as that thought slid through his mind, he corrected it firmly.

"Not a *fault*," he muttered thickly, shifting his gaze away from the house where his family gathered without him, *"a choice."*

He was here, wasn't he? He'd come back to the place that still haunted his dreams and he'd given his word to stay the rest of the summer. Coming out to the barn didn't mean he was leaving. He'd just needed some time. Some peace. Some space. To think. To figure out what to do.

So he'd left the house, turning his back on the family he was just rediscovering and come out to the barn to work on his bike. It soothed him, tinkering with the engine, making minute adjustments. Always had. He could lose himself in an engine and let the rest of the world drift away.

Jake set the socket wrench back in the toolbox, then tucked the box into the bike's steel saddlebag. He was relieved that Jeremiah was healthy. And it was damn good to see Sam and Cooper again, too. But being back in Coleville was harder than he'd thought it was going to be.

And it had gotten even harder a half hour ago, when Jeremiah had made his grand announcement. Just remembering those quietly spoken words had Jake's blood quickening. He wavered between temper and regret. Feelings he had way too much familiarity with.

His gaze flicked over the dimly lit barn, swept across his motorcycle one last time, and then Jake was moving. He had to move. Couldn't stand still while his brain raced. Couldn't think while memories rushed through his mind, making it hard to breathe.

Shaking his head, Jake stalked out of the barn, turned right and kept walking until he was halfway across the ranch yard. Then he stopped dead, like a man unsure of where to go next. Moonlight shone down from a starlit sky, illuminating the yard and the acres of land that stretched out on either side of the old house.

His mind raced, replaying over and over again Jeremiah's bombshell announcement.

Donna Barrett's back in town—and she's brought Mac's son with her.

Jake started walking again, headed for the rail fence that surrounded the yard and separated it from the fields. When he reached it, he grabbed hold with both hands, and held on tight, as if needing that grip on something solid to keep him balanced.

"Mac's *son*," he whispered, voice breaking as he let his head fall back and his gaze fix on the distant stars. The rough wood bit into his palms and he welcomed the scrape of discomfort.

Around him, open land lay fallow, the fields empty at this time of year. A mile or more away, golden squares outlined the windows of the home of Jeremiah's closest neighbor. And in the distance, a dog barked.

He inhaled sharply, deeply, drawing the cool night air into lungs that felt squeezed by the tightness of his chest. Heart hammering, he swallowed hard and lowered his gaze to the familiarity of the Lonergan ranch. Jake knew every inch of this place. He'd spent every summer of his childhood on this ranch, running wild with his cousins. Four

Lonergan boys looking for trouble, he remembered. Until that last summer.

He couldn't believe this. Fifteen years he'd been gone from Coleville, California. Fifteen years, he'd stayed away from this place, his cousins and the grandfather he loved. Because he hadn't been able to deal with the memories of that one last summer. Now, to find out that there was even more going on back then than he'd thought, was almost too much to take in.

Whether he wanted it or not, the trickle of memories became a flood, filling his mind, his senses, overcoming him before he could stop them. He stared into the surrounding blackness, but saw instead, the past.

Days were long and the sun blazed down from a brassy sky. Summers stretched out forever and there was nothing more to worry about than who won the daily challenge at the lake.

And Jake wasn't even worried about that. He always won. He liked winning. He was good at it.

That last morning, they lined up on the ridge above the ranch lake. The competition was simple. Jumping for distance into the icy cold water, then staying beneath the surface as long as possible.

They took turns, the four Lonergan boys, jumping off the ridge into the water. The contest was not just about distance reached on those jumps, though, it was also about how long you stayed underwater holding your breath.

Jake felt cold rivulets of water streaming from his long hair, rolling down his chest. He squinted into the sunlight glancing off the surface of the lake and watched for air bubbles. Temper seething, he cussed up a storm as he waited for Mac to finish his turn. His jump had matched Jake's, now all that was left was staying underwater longer.

But he wouldn't. Not one of them could hold their breath as long as Jake could.

Damn it.

Sam was worried, kept saying they should go in after Mac, because he'd never stayed down that long.

"Give him another minute, Sam," Cooper said. "He really wants to beat Jake. And I want him to. Mac's okay. Stop being an old lady."

Jake's temper frothed and every swear word he'd ever learned came pouring from his mouth. He couldn't believe Mac stood a chance of actually beating him. Damn it.

"We'll give him another thirty seconds," Sam said, grinning. "He keeps this up, he's gonna beat Jake's best time."

His fists tightening on the split rail fence sent a jagged sliver of wood into his palm and the sharp pain jolted Jake from his memories. Just as well. Wasn't a day he enjoyed reliving.

Though God knew, he saw it often enough in his dreams.

Emotions churned so quickly inside him that he couldn't even identify them all, but he knew they were strangling him. He half turned and looked back over his shoulder at the house. Lamplight spilled from every window. Through the kitchen curtains, he could see his family, apparently still reeling from Jeremiah's little news flash. Jake probably should have stayed with them, talked this all out. But what was there to say?

They all knew what they had to do. There was nothing to talk about. Nothing to decide.

Mac had a *son.*

End of story.

Even as he thought that, the back door opened, light sliced through the moonlit shadows and his cousins Sam and Cooper stepped outside. Only took them a moment to spot him and then they were headed toward him.

Jake released his grip on the fence and turned around to lean against the railings. The sting of the sliver nagged at his palm, but he folded his arms over his chest as he waited for his cousins to reach him. A wind kicked dust into the air, blew it around a bit, then set it back down again before moving on.

Jeremiah's new golden retriever puppy, Sheba, shot through the slowly closing back door and scrambled down the short set of steps to the dirt.

She raced after Sam and Cooper and wriggled gleefully when Sam bent down, scooped her up and tucked her into the crook of his arm.

As they came closer, Jake watched their faces, seeing the stamp of familiarity there. The three of them looked a lot alike—their grandmother, Jeremiah's late wife, used to say they all had the "Lonergan look." Dark hair, dark eyes, stubborn jaw and hard heads.

God, Jake had missed these guys.

The cousins had once been as close as brothers. And the fifteen years since he'd seen Sam and Cooper had been the loneliest of his life. Still, he wasn't exactly in the mood to talk. Not even to these two.

"I came out here to be alone," Jake said, though he knew it wouldn't do any good. His cousins would come and go as they pleased. Just as he always did.

"Yeah, well," Sam said, lifting his chin to avoid puppy kisses, "you're *not* alone. So get used to it."

He didn't think he could.

Alone was better.

Easier.

"We need to figure out what to do," Cooper said.

Not surprising to hear him say that. Cooper always was the one who liked a good plan. Probably came in handy when he was writing those horror novels of his. Coop's novels had been hitting bestseller lists for the last few years, and were probably responsible for half the nightmares in America.

"What's to figure out?" Jake asked, pushing away from the fence to brace his legs wide apart in an unconscious battle stance. "Mac has a son. The kid's a Lonergan. One of us."

"Ease up," Sam said, setting the dog down to race in circles around the yard. He shook his head at the little dog, then shifted a look at Jake. "All I'm saying is we shouldn't go racing over there to welcome the kid into the family."

"Why the hell not?" Temper flashed inside Jake, but he tried to squelch it. "We *owe* him. Owe Mac."

"Damn it, Jake," Sam snapped, "you're not the only one who feels terrible here, you know? But that doesn't mean we go barging in on Donna and force our way into *her* kid's life."

"Who said anything about forcing?" Jake argued. "I'm just saying we should go see him. Talk to him. Tell him about Mac. About what he meant to us. What's wrong with that?"

"God, Jake. Maybe the kid doesn't even know he's a Lonergan," Cooper said quietly. "We don't know what Donna's told him. Or what she doesn't want him to know."

That hit him like a two-by-four. Jake sucked in a gulp of air and swallowed it, holding it down like he was preparing for another run and jump into the lake. *Of course Donna would have told the kid about Mac.* Wouldn't she? He scraped one hand across his face and blew out the air he'd been holding.

"Fine. I go see Donna."

"You mean *we* go see Donna," Sam corrected, and whistled for the dog that was racing toward the barn.

"I mean *me*. Alone," Jake said, glancing from one cousin to the other, to make sure that both of them understood this. "I'll talk to her."

"And why are you elected?" Cooper asked.

Good question, he thought. But he couldn't give them an answer. At least not the one that mattered. Instead he said, "You and Sam have got other things to do," he pointed out. "He's got his new medical practice, you're probably in the middle of another book—"

"So?" Cooper asked.

"So, you've got Maggie and Kara to think about, too. I don't." Lame, but the best he could come up with at the moment. "I'll go see Donna. See the kid. Then the three of us can decide what to do."

Sheba raced up, barking her head off, looking for some attention and Jake was grateful for the distraction. Both of his cousins watched him carefully for another moment or two, then nodded.

"Fine," Sam said. "But you don't talk to the kid without us there. We're all in this. Together."

Together was a word Jake hadn't had a lot of use for in the last fifteen years. A man alone did what he wanted, when he wanted and didn't have to concern himself with anyone else. But now he was back in Coleville and things were different.

At least for a while.

"What do you mean, 'you have a date'?" Donna Barrett blinked and looked at her mother as though she'd never seen her before.

Her mother? Dating?

"Now think about it, honey," her mother said, glancing into the mirror over her left shoulder to check that her black skirt was hanging just right. "How many things could I possibly mean?"

Donna flopped down onto the end of her mother's bed. The handmade quilt covering the old double mattress felt soft and cool against her bare thighs. Even in the air-conditioned house, summer in Coleville, California, was hot enough to make wearing shorts a necessity.

Shaking her head, she watched her mom, Catherine, preen and primp like a teenager getting ready for the prom. Leaning into the mirror, the older woman touched up her lipstick, then fluffed her short, auburn hair. Smiling knowingly into the glass, she said, "Your dad's been gone two years, baby."

Donna sighed. True. Jeff Barrett, a healthy, robust man of fifty-five had dropped dead of a sudden heart attack two years ago. Donna was still living in Colorado then. Her mother had insisted that she was fine and that Donna should go on with her life.

And she had. At least, she'd tried, keeping in touch with near-daily phone calls and several visits. Until finally, a couple of months ago, she'd overridden her mother's objections and moved back home. And though Catherine hadn't wanted to admit it, the relief in her face had told Donna all she'd needed to know.

She'd had to come home—for a lot of reasons. But that didn't make being here any easier. Especially now, with two of the Lonergan boys back in town. She'd already run into Cooper at the drugstore. And with Sam the new town doctor, she'd certainly be seeing him sooner or later.

And Sam would be seeing *Eric*.

At the thought of her son, Donna chewed frantically at her bottom lip. There was no going back, now. She was home, for good. Better for her mom. Better for her. Better for Eric. It was just the settling in, finding their way that was so damn hard.

For so long, it had been just the two of them. And now, everything was changing.

Oh, God.

She felt as though she were on a broken Ferris wheel, spinning continually, first up, then down, then up again. Her stomach churned and every breath felt like a battle well fought.

Her mother was watching her, worry in her

eyes, so Donna pushed her thoughts to one side and tried to smile. "Hard to believe Daddy's been gone so long already."

"Nice attempt," her mother said softly. "But you weren't just thinking about your dad."

"Yes, I was," Donna said. "About dad and Mac and Eric and…everything. I guess," she added with a helpless smile, "I just don't like change."

"I know," Catherine said, her gaze shifting to the small, framed photo of Jeff Barrett, standing on the dressing table. "Took forever for me to actually believe your dad was really gone. Sometimes I still expect to hear him calling to me from the other room."

Great. Way to go, Donna. Depress your mother just before her big night out. "Well, if he were here, he'd be the first to tell you that you look great."

Catherine smiled. Mission accomplished.

"So how long have you been dating this guy? And just what do we know about him?"

"Very funny," her mother said dryly. "And I know all I need to know. I started seeing Michael six months ago."

"Six months ago?" Donna stared blankly. "And I'm just hearing about this now because…"

"Because I thought—silly me—that you might take it badly." Catherine's lips twitched.

Outside, the neighbor's dog barked at the moon and the sprinkler hissed and stuttered as it shot water across the wide lawn. Cool air whispered from the overhead vents and seconds ticked by as Donna tried to come to grips with a single fact.

Her mother had more of a social life than *she* did.

"I'm just…surprised, is all," Donna hedged. "Who is this Michael person and why haven't I met him? I've been home two months, you know."

Catherine laughed and her deep blue eyes, so much like Donna's own, sparkled. "We haven't seen much of each other since you got home. I wanted to give you a chance to settle in before…" Her voice trailed off, then picked up again. "Besides, you have met him. It's Michael Cochran, honey."

"Mr. *Cochran?*" Donna yelped, jumping off the edge of the mattress. "My biology teacher?"

Catherine picked up her bag, opened it and stuffed in her wallet and lipstick before saying, "He's not your teacher anymore."

"Yeah, but—"

"Donna—" her mother's tone changed slightly "—I'm delighted you've come home, honey. But Michael hasn't been your teacher in fifteen years."

"True," Donna said, sinking back down to the foot of the bed again. "It's just…*weird,*" she added. "Thinking about you going out with someone who isn't, well, *Dad.*"

Catherine smiled a little and took a seat beside her daughter. Draping one arm around her shoulders, she said, "It was hard for me, too. At first.

But whether we like it or not, honey, life goes on. And I'm tired of being lonely. You understand, don't you?"

Lonely? Oh, yeah. Donna understood lonely.

And scared.

And worried.

"Sure I do," she said. "I was just…surprised. That's all."

Her mom gave her a tight hug, then sprang up when the doorbell rang. Shooting a glance at the open doorway, she said, "That'll be Michael."

"Have a good time," Donna said, forcing a smile she really didn't feel. Not an easy thing, seeing your mother go off on a date. Especially with your old teacher.

"You sure you'll be all right?"

Donna rolled her eyes. "Yes, *Mom.* I'm fine. Eric and I will order pizza or something. Go. Have fun."

"I'll see you later," Catherine said with a wave as she scurried out of her bedroom, headed for the front door.

"Right." Alone, Donna just sat there for a long minute, staring at her own reflection in her mother's mirror.

Nothing stayed the same, she knew that better than anyone. But did *everything* have to change at *once?*

When the phone rang, she scrambled up off the bed and hurried into the hall to pick up the extension. Probably Eric begging to stay a little longer at the miniature golf palace.

Snatching up the phone, she was already smiling as she said, "Hello, Eric."

"Wrong Lonergan, Donna," the deep voice rumbling in her ear said. "This is Jake."

Two

"Donna?" Jake asked. "You still there?"

The silence on the other end of the line stretched out for what felt like forever. Laughter and bits of conversation drifted to him from the living room where the rest of the family was gathered. Here in the kitchen, though, Jake stood at the window, looking out into the night, trying to imagine Donna's face.

An image of her the last time he'd seen her popped up in his brain and he almost wished it hadn't. She walked across the cemetery, weaving in and out of the headstones decorated by wilting bouquets. Her steps were slow, unsure, shaky. Her head was bent, her long blond hair hanging down on either side of her face like a soft curtain designed to keep the world out. She stopped alongside him on the way to her parents' car and lifted her face to him.

Jake felt again, that punch of helplessness as she'd looked up at him through blue eyes, red from crying. Fresh tears tracked across her pale cheeks and shone in the sunlight. Her full lips pressed firmly together, she didn't speak. She only looked at him for a long minute before turning and walking away. Standing alone, Jake could only stare after her.

Two weeks later, she'd left Coleville without telling a soul where she was going.

"What do you want, Jake?" she finally asked, dragging him back from the past.

"Jeremiah told us." He deliberately pushed old memories down into the deep, dark hole he'd dug for them years before. "About Mac's son."

She sucked in air and the soft hissing sound teased his ear. "*My* son," she corrected.

"Of course he's your son, too," he said, and his voice sounded harsher than he'd meant it. He slapped one hand to the wall and winced as the sliver still embedded in his palm dug a little deeper. He leaned in closer to the window, stared past his own reflection in the glass, to watch the sky. A falling star sliced across the blackness leaving a trail of fire behind it. He closed his eyes, searched for calm and tried again. "I only wanted to say that we know about him now and we want—"

Before he could finish, Donna interrupted.

"I really don't care what you guys want, Jake."

"Well, good to know we're going to be reasonable."

"I'm plenty reasonable. I didn't call you," she reminded him hotly.

"No, you sure as hell didn't," Jake accused. "Not then. Not now."

She blew out an impatient breath. "Look, I know you probably mean well…"

"Probably?" He took the phone from his ear, stared at it, stunned, then slapped it back into place. "I *probably* mean well?"

"Fine. You mean well. But I don't need anything from you. My *son* doesn't need anything from you."

"You don't have to jump down my throat," he countered, "I was only—"

"What?" she demanded. "You were only *what,* exactly?"

"Damn it, why're you being so bitchy about this?"

"Bitchy? Excuse me?"

"I didn't mean—"

"Yeah, you did. And you can just back off, Jake Lonergan. I don't have to explain myself to you."

Shaking his head, he cursed himself mentally

for clearly going about this all wrong. He should have remembered what a hard head Donna had. Should have tried to be calm. Should have tried to talk to her without starting World War III.

"You're making this harder than it has to be," he said on a tired sigh.

"It doesn't have to be *anything,* Jake," she told him. "Just because I'm home doesn't mean that I'm looking to share my son with the Lonergan cousins."

"Well that's too damn bad, isn't it?" he countered quickly, forgetting all about trying to be calm. Hell, just hearing her voice again after all these years was enough to get rid of any chance for "calm."

Turning away from the window, he leaned one hip against the wall, and fixed his gaze on the ceiling. Inhaling sharply, he tightened his grip on the phone receiver, and managed, through a great use of will, to keep his voice even. "The kid is one of *us.* He deserves to know it."

"The *kid,*" she emphasized the word he'd used and Jake muffled a groan. "His *name* is Eric. And he *knows* who his father was," she said quietly. "I've told him all about Mac."

"Ah, God." A knot of pain lodged in Jake's throat and he grimly swallowed it. The swinging door from the living room opened and Sam stepped into the kitchen, his dark gaze locking on Jake. Jake scowled at him and jerked his head at the door, telling his cousin silently to get out. Sam planted his feet and shook his head.

So Jake ignored him.

"Donna," he said, lowering his voice to a whisper, "we just want to talk to him."

She was quiet for a long time. Long enough that Jake was almost convinced she'd set the phone down and walked away.

"I'll think about it." One quick sentence, then she hung up.

A dial tone rang in his ear and Jake ground his back teeth together. Slowly he walked back to the wall phone and hung up the receiver carefully.

"So," Sam observed wryly, "that went well."

"Butt out."

"Yeah, because you're doing so great."

Jake snapped him a look that should have fried him on the spot. Sam was unmoved.

"Don't try the black look on me, bud. I've known you too long."

Jake blew out a frustrated breath and rubbed one hand viciously against the back of his neck. He shrugged and admitted, "She didn't want to talk to me."

"Not a big surprise, is it?" Sam asked, walking past Jake to the refrigerator.

"Well, yeah," Jake said, "it is. Why wouldn't she want to talk to me?"

Sam opened the fridge, rummaged around

inside and kept talking, his voice muffled. "Not just you. I'm thinking any of us would have gotten that reaction. Hell, Jake, she's been hiding Mac's son from us for fifteen years. Any big shocker that she'd like to keep on doing it?"

"Guess not." He leaned back against the kitchen counter and crossed one booted foot over the other. Folding his arms across his chest, he waited for Sam to straighten up and close the fridge with his hip before saying, "But she's gotta know we're not going to go along with that. Not now that we know."

"Sure she does. Doesn't mean she's happy about it." He held the necks of two beer bottles in each hand. "It's just going to take some patience. A little finesse."

"I can do finesse."

Sam snorted. "Right."

Frowning, Jake pushed away from the counter and shoved both hands into his jeans pockets. "I'll take care of it."

Sam just stared at him for a long minute, then said, "Fine. We'll wait for you to screw it up, then we'll step in."

"Thanks for the vote of confidence."

Sam chuckled. "No offense, Jake, but you never have been long on patience."

No point in arguing that, he thought, and said nothing as Sam left the kitchen to rejoin the family in the living room. He'd never been a patient man. He'd gotten a grip on his flash fire temper years ago, but the impatient streak was still there.

That sense of urgency had served him well on the professional racing circuit. He'd stayed ahead of the pack by pushing the limits, by expecting more from his custom built motorcycles than the other players did. But Sam was right. Impatient wasn't going to work on Donna.

He wished he knew what the hell would.

"Did you hear? Jake Lonergan's back in town."

Donna jolted at the sound of his name, but kept her smile fixed and firm as she met Margie Fontenot's cool blue gaze. The older woman had lived her entire life in Coleville and her grapevine was always buzzing. Nothing happened in this town that Margie didn't hear about.

"I heard."

"Not surprised," Margie said, handing over a DVD copy of her favorite musical. "Town's talking about nothing else. Imagine those Lonergan boys finally coming home. Jake was the last one to arrive, you know. Saw him myself two days ago, big as life, rolling down Main Street on a motorcycle loud enough to wake the dead."

"That sounds like Jake all right," Donna managed to say despite the huge knot suddenly tightening up in the middle of her throat. She wondered how she'd missed seeing Jake on his motorcycle. And wondered why she was sorry she had.

Her fingers shook as she picked up the DVD, ran the bar code over the scanner and said, "That's two dollars even for a five day rental, Margie."

"More than fair," the older woman said, digging into a "pocketbook" as big as a suitcase. She finally came up with a wildly flowered change purse, which she opened to pour out a stream of quarters, nickels and dimes across the counter. "You know," she continued as she systematically counted out the correct amount of change, "the Lonergan boys were always a wild bunch. Used to tell Jeremiah to draw a tight rein on 'em, but he never could. Just loved watching the four of those boys together."

The *four*.

A sharp, sweet ache settled in Donna's chest and her breath caught at the familiarity of the sensation.

Years ago, there had been four Lonergan cousins, Donna remembered, her memories sweeping over her while Margie Fontenot chattered away. Sam, Cooper, Mac and Jake. Fifteen years ago, she herself had been a part of their exclusive group. Mostly because of Mac. She smiled now, remembering the then sixteen-year-old boy's easy grin and kind eyes.

"Of course," Margie said on a sigh, "after the tragedy, nothing was ever quite the same again."

Her eyes narrowed thoughtfully. "But you know that better than most, don't you dear?"

"I guess maybe I do," Donna agreed vaguely, refusing to give Margie any more gossip than she'd already picked up. The older woman had, more than likely, come into the video rental store only to get more fodder for her grapevine.

The other ladies in town were probably dying to find out what was going to happen now that Donna had brought her son home. One look at Eric and his parentage was no secret. Her son was absolutely the picture of Mac at that age. There could be no doubt who the boy's father had been.

He had Lonergan dark eyes and hair and the same quick grin Mac had flashed all the time. He stood like Mac, moved like Jake, had the imagination of Cooper and was as smart as Sam.

But her son had his mother's heart.

And Donna would do whatever she had to do to protect him from pain.

"Now, honey," Margie said, stretching out one well-manicured hand to pat Donna. "Don't you worry about a thing."

"I'm not worried, Margie."

"That's good, then. No need, you know. It's time your boy got to know his family."

Donna inhaled slowly, deeply and told herself that the older woman meant well. "Thanks. I'll keep that in mind."

"You always were a good girl, Donna."

Grabbing up her huge purse, Margie clutched her rented movie and swept through the front door. Donna blew out a breath, steadied herself then hustled out from behind the counter. Wandering up and down the aisles, she straightened movie jackets, plucking sci-fi flicks out of romantic comedy and cartoons out of horror.

Shaking her head, she returned everything to their proper places and tried not to think about what Margie had said. Or, about that phone call from Jake last night. Better if she just concentrated on running the shop her parents had started so long ago. Better if she kept reminding herself that she hadn't only returned to Coleville because her mom was alone. But because Eric was getting older. Needing a man in his life. Needing…more than she was able to give him.

Oh, how it stung to admit that.

Behind her, the front door swung open and the cowbell her father had hung so many years ago jangled a greeting. Donna turned and grinned.

"Hi, Mom," Eric shouted, snatching up a candy bar from the display by the cash register.

"Hey, did you have lunch?" she automatically asked.

"Yeah," he said, peeling back the brightly colored wrap and taking a bite of chocolate. "Grandma took me out for a burger." While he talked, he glanced through the stack of returned movies that hadn't been returned to the shelves yet. *"Cool,"* he shouted, holding up a copy of what looked like some bloodthirsty slasher movie. "Can I take this home?"

"A world of no," she said, coming up close enough to snatch the movie from his grip, and then take a bite of his candy bar. "Rated 'R,' bud," she said, then grimaced at the bloody picture.

"What good does it do me to have access to all these movies if you won't let me watch the ones I want to?" he asked, already moving into the horror section.

"It's a hard, hard life," Donna said, smiling as she watched her son stoop to check out the bottom shelf.

There were a lot of things in her life that she might regret, she thought, but Eric would never be one of them. He was her heart. Her reason. The one part of her world that always made sense to her.

He looked at her and gave her a grin. "That's what *I* keep saying. But does anybody listen?"

"Funny." Shaking her head, she turned again when the front door opened and this time, she didn't smile. This time, her breath caught in her chest and her heartbeat stuttered wildly. "Jake."

He seemed to take up the whole doorway. His shoulders were broad, his waist narrow and his legs looked about three miles long. He wore a white T-shirt, black jeans and scuffed up, square toed boots. He still wore his black hair long and pulled into a low ponytail at the back of his neck. Sunglasses hid his eyes from her, and maybe that was just as well.

But as soon as she thought that, he pulled the glasses off and hooked them in the neck of his shirt. Those dark eyes fixed on her and a rush of heat swept through her body. A curl of something delicious unwound in the pit of her stomach, and a little farther south, her body started tingling.

"Donna. You look good."

"I feel good," she said, swallowing hard.

"Yeah," he countered with a slow smile. "I remember."

Three

Donna's blue eyes went wide and a hot rush of color filled her cheeks. Her breath caught in her lungs and Jake watched as she bit down hard on her bottom lip. A light tugging sensation developing deep inside him.

"Don't," she whispered, shaking her head and taking a slow step back for good measure.

"Donna…" Even the air-conditioning in the store, turned up to just below freezing, couldn't put out the fire engulfing him. Every cell in his body hummed and he could almost *feel* electricity arcing out around the two of them.

Damn.

He'd had no idea that just seeing her again would hit him this hard. Should've known, though. Should've remembered what she'd been able to do to him fifteen years ago with a simple look.

Back then, she'd haunted every one of his dreams and tormented him every day. He hadn't been able to avoid her, even if he'd wanted to—because she'd been Mac's girlfriend.

So he'd suffered in silence, hungering for her as only a seventeen-year-old boy could hunger. She was every thought, every desire, every need. And she'd been unattainable.

Until one night that last summer.

She'd only been a kid, then. Fifteen and the most beautiful thing he'd ever seen. Now, she was a woman and she took his breath away.

"Jake, you shouldn't have come here."

"I just want to talk, Donna," he said, stepping closer to the counter she kept between them like a shield. That was a lie, he thought. He wanted to do *way* more than just talk. His mind filled with images of everything he wanted to do—*with* her and *to* her. His body tightened until he nearly groaned aloud.

Then watching as her eyes flashed with worry, he snapped, "Relax, okay? I won't bite." The tension in her shoulders eased up until he added, "Unless you want me to."

"Cut it out." She glanced over her shoulder and Jake followed her look.

He spotted the boy instantly. A teenager, crouched down to inspect the movies lined up on the bottom shelf. As he grabbed one and straightened up, Jake took the kid's measure. Tall and lean, the boy had black hair, dark eyes and a curious expression on his face.

Jake felt a blow to his solar plexus. The boy looked just like Mac had that last summer. God, it was like stepping back in time. The ache he'd felt for Donna faded into an ache of regret.

"How about this one, Mom?" the boy asked as he approached the counter. "No blood, but there's ghosts and stuff." He glanced at Jake. "Hi."

"Hi."

"Fine," Donna said quickly, forcing a smile that only Jake seemed to notice was phony. "Take it on back to the house, honey. Tell Grandma I'll pick up chicken for dinner."

"Cool," he said, "but can I have five bucks? I'm supposed to meet Jason at the deli and…"

"Sure," she said, not even waiting for the whole explanation. She hit a key on the cash register and when the drawer slid out, she snatched up a five-dollar bill, and handed it over.

"That was easy," the kid said, then shot Jake a grin as he left.

The cowbell jangled for a full minute before falling into silence. Jake was still standing there looking after the boy when Donna spoke up.

"You've seen Eric now, so why don't you go, Jake?"

He turned his head to stare into her eyes. Eyes he'd been seeing in his sleep for fifteen years. "He looks just like him."

"I know."

Jake scraped one hand across his face. "He didn't know who I was."

"Why would he?" she countered and started stacking returned movies in alphabetical order. "He's never seen you before, Jake."

That stung.

His gaze swept the interior of the store. Hadn't changed much over the years. There were more DVDs than VHS tapes now, but the setup was the same. The walls had been painted a stark white and movie posters dotted almost every surface. Windows facing onto Main Street gleamed in the sunlight and an action adventure movie was playing on the TV at the end of the counter.

He sighed, shifted his gaze back to Donna and said quietly, "If we'd known about him, things would have been different."

Her hands stilled on the movie cases and she lifted her gaze to his. "I know that. But I did what I had to do."

"Alone?"

"I wasn't alone," she said and went back to her

work. "I had my aunt Lily. She was…" Donna stopped and smiled, *"wonderful."*

Glad to hear she hadn't been completely alone, Jake tried to imagine her as she must have been back then. Just a kid. Pregnant. Far from home. The father of her child, dead.

Pain lanced through him like a blade, then disappeared under the onslaught of the familiar ache he'd carried with him for years.

As if reading his thoughts, she said softly, "It was a long time ago, Jake."

"Yeah, sometimes it feels like another lifetime," he admitted. "And sometimes it feels like yesterday."

Donna braced herself and lifted her gaze to his again. He'd surprised her before. No doubt that was the reason she'd gone so hot the instant she caught sight of him. Well, that and the sound of his voice rumbling over her, reminding her of that night when everything in her life had changed forever.

Inhaling sharply, deeply, she picked up a stack of movies and walked out from behind the counter, moving into the widely spaced aisles. She wasn't surprised at all to hear Jake's heavy boot steps right behind her. *Concentrate on work,* she told herself. *The movies.* She slid a romantic comedy alphabetically into place in the sci-fi section and muttered under her breath when he plucked it off the shelf.

"Wrong spot."

"I knew that."

He snorted. "So you were just testing *me?*"

"No," she said, grabbing the movie back from him and quickly moving around to the correct aisle. "I'm trying to work here, Jake. So why don't you just go?"

"Not before we talk."

She stopped, slapped the movie into the correct slot, then turned to look at him. But even braced for the impact of his gaze, she felt the jolt of a nearly electrical sexual energy. *Oh, boy.*

"We have talked. You've seen Eric. Now go."

"Seen him. Haven't met him. Haven't talked to him." He moved in closer to her and Donna would have bet that she could actually *feel* his body heat rippling off of him in waves. "Not going anywhere until I do."

God, he took up so much *room.*

She had to tip her head back to meet his gaze squarely. He was tall, taller than she remembered. And his shoulders were broader now, his chest more muscular. His hair was still thick and long, making her want to tear the leather cord off his ponytail and run her fingers through his hair. His strong jaw was shadowed with whiskers and his dark brows were drawn together as he studied her.

He was even more tempting now than he'd been as a teenager. And back then, Donna had never been more tempted by anything than she had been by Jake Lonergan.

Stalling for time to think, Donna turned around abruptly and walked to the drama aisle. There she slid four movies into the proper slots before continuing on to the children's section. Jake stayed just a step or two behind her.

She felt him watching her. Felt his gaze on her until her spine twitched and her blood pumped. Something deep inside her flickered wildly into life and a part of her welcomed it even as she tried to ignore it.

"So you're running the shop now, huh?"

Donna tossed him a quick glance over her shoulder. "Don't miss much, do you Jake?"

"Cute." He ran the tip of one finger along the top of the shelf as he walked. "But I figured you'd be a teacher by now."

"What?" She stopped at the classic movie aisle and turned to look at him again.

"Teaching? You?" He smiled and Donna's insides went on a roller-coaster ride. "You used to talk about being a teacher."

"You remember that?"

"I remember *everything,*" Jake said softly.

She closed her eyes, figuring it was safer than maintaining eye contact with Jake. Unfortunately, while she wasn't looking, he moved in even closer. The instant he dropped his hands onto her shoulders, her eyes flew open and she swayed unsteadily toward him. A half smile on his face gave her the strength to lock her knees and straighten up.

She stepped out from under his grasp and shook her head clear of the sensations sparking in her brain. "You have to stop saying things like that."

"Why?"

"Because we're not kids anymore, Jake. Times have changed. *I've* changed."

He shoved his hands into his jeans pockets. "So have I."

Donna laughed shortly and gave him a slow look up and down. "No, you haven't," she said. "You're still danger man."

"What?"

"Oh, please. Look at you, Jake. The long hair, the scruffy whiskers, the battered boots and faded jeans—not to mention the motorcycle that's no doubt parked outside. You're the *poster* boy for danger."

"Yeah?" His smile grew a little broader and a pleased gleam shone in his eyes.

"That wasn't a compliment." But of course it *was*. God, even though she'd been crazy about Mac as a kid, Jake had fueled way too many of her dreams. Even then, he'd been able to get to her like no one else ever had.

And apparently, that hadn't changed any with the passing of the years.

"So I worry you?" he prodded.

"On an elemental level," she admitted, "yes."

"Good to know."

"Figures you'd like hearing that."

"What man wouldn't?"

"Mac," she said, and instantly, the humor in his eyes drained away and tension erupted between them.

"Fine." Jake nodded abruptly. "You want to talk about Mac? Let's do it. After Mac died—" he swallowed hard as if even the words themselves tasted bitter "—when you found out you were pregnant, why didn't you tell *me* at least?"

"I couldn't."

"We were friends." He paused. "*More* than friends."

Heat flooded her system, sweeping up from the soles of her feet right up and through the top of her head. Memories were suddenly so thick she could hardly breathe. She remembered it all, too, as clearly as Jake did.

"That's why I couldn't tell you."

"Damn it, Donna," he said, reaching for her, grabbing her upper arms and pulling her close so quickly, she dropped the movies she still held and they clattered to the floor at their feet. "You shouldn't have cut me out."

She yanked free of his grip, bent down, snatched up the fallen movies and clutched them to her chest. "I didn't owe you anything, Jake. Not any of you guys. Eric wasn't *your* son, he was Mac's. The only one I owed was Mac and he was gone."

Oh, God. Tears blurred her vision, making her furious. She didn't want to cry in front of him. Didn't want to cry again at all. She'd spilled enough tears that summer to last her a lifetime.

"I could have helped."

"You were seventeen."

"I—"

"Jake, be realistic," she said, tired now, "you'd already enlisted in the Marine Corps. You were on your way to boot camp. I had a baby to think of. To plan for."

He blew out an impatient breath but she could see that he wasn't willing to let go of this. He was still caught in the decisions made that long-ago summer. But then, wasn't she? She had a living, breathing reminder with her every day of her life.

"You have to let this go, Jake. Just go back to your life and—"

"And what? Forget about Eric now that I know about him?" He shook his head. "Not gonna happen."

"No, I guess it's not," she said, sighing. "But if you and the others want to get to know Eric, it's going to be on my terms. He's *my* son and I have to do what I think is best for him."

"Agreed," he said quickly.

"To quote my son," she said warily, "that was easy."

"Relax," he told her. "I'm not planning anything. I just want to make this as easy as possible on all of us."

"And all of a sudden, you're Mr. Reasonable?"

"Maybe he'll worry you less than Mr. Danger."

Donna gave him a reluctant smile. Jake had always been able to talk his way around a problem. "Wouldn't count on that. At least with Mr. Danger I know where I stand."

"Where's that?" he asked, bending in closer, leaning his head down until they were nearly eye to eye.

"On the edge of a very steep cliff," she said, meeting his gaze and not backing down.

"Is that why you ran that night?"

She didn't have to ask him which night he meant. Over the years, that one particular memory had haunted her. She'd often wondered what might have happened, what might have been different if she hadn't run from Jake in a blind panic.

He ran one hand along her arm and tingles of awareness, expectation, shot off in her bloodstream like fireworks. Donna sucked in a gulp of air and held it, as if half afraid she'd never be able to draw another.

"Did I really scare you off?" he asked, his voice soft, intimate. "I would never have hurt you, Donna."

She lifted one hand to cover his, still on her arm. "I know that, Jake. I knew that then, too."

"Then why?" he asked, voice now raw with a need she recognized. "If you weren't scared of me...why did you run away that night?"

"I wasn't afraid of you, Jake," Donna admitted, looking up into his eyes, losing herself in the dark depths swirling with emotions they shouldn't have reawakened. "I ran that night because I was afraid of *me*. Of what you made me feel."

Sunlight glanced in through the wide windows overlooking Main Street and nearly blinded her. Her eyes teared and she wasn't sure why. Was it the memories? Jake's touch? Or just the searing sunlight?

"So what we felt when we kissed," he whispered, "the passion, the desire...you ran from all of that—left me alone and went straight to Mac."

"Yes," she said tightly.

"Did you sleep with him that night?" The question came out in a snarl, but Donna heard the hurt beneath the temper and responded to that.

"Yeah, Jake. I did." She met his gaze, lifted her chin and told him what she'd never told anyone else before. "I found passion with you, but ran to Mac. And that night, we made Eric."

Four

In an instant, Jake was there again, that hot, summer night fifteen years ago.

The scent of her filled him. Her heat washed over him and made his seventeen-year-old heart pound with a fierce drumbeat in his chest. Moonlight danced in her eyes as her teeth tugged at her bottom lip.

Jake's cousins were off at the lake, swimming. It was just he and Donna now, standing on the side of the road beside her father's car. He'd left the house later than the other guys, wanting some time alone. When he spotted the car broken down on the side of the road, he'd recognized both it and the driver.

He told himself that Donna was Mac's girl, but it didn't seem to help. All he could think of was how much he wanted her. How much he cared for her.

Fighting back the urge to reach out and grab her, he instead walked to the front of the car and opened the hood. Donna came and stood beside him and her perfume wrapped itself around him like a heavy cloak.

"Can you fix it?" she asked, her voice soft.

"Yeah," he muttered, spotting the problem right away. "Distributor wire's come loose."

He didn't want to fix it. Didn't want to help her get in the car and drive off to meet Mac. He wanted her here. With him. Gritting his teeth, Jake leaned in, grabbed hold of the wire and adjusted the connection. He fiddled around a few extra, precious seconds, checking other wires needlessly, anything to keep her here beside him.

Donna moved up closer and tripped, falling against his side. In a reflex action, Jake grabbed her, steadied her, then instead of letting her go, wrapped his arms around her, pulling her closer.

"Jake…" She swallowed hard and looked up at him. "I should—"

"—go," he finished for her. "Yeah, I know."

Jake had known Donna for years. And they'd always been friends. This summer, though, something had changed. Though she was Mac's girlfriend, Jake had felt her watching him when she thought he wasn't looking. He'd seen the same interest in her eyes that he knew shone in his.

There was something between them. Something he wanted to explore. Something he wanted defined. Did she feel for him what he felt for her?

Was it possible that she didn't love Mac? Could she love him instead?

Her hands flattened on his chest and he knew she felt his heartbeat pounding frantically. Her touch seemed to sear him right down to his bones. Heat rushed through his body, staggering him with the force of the desire nearly choking him.

"Donna," he whispered, bending his head down to hers, "don't go. Stay. With me."

She shook her head slowly. "I can't. You know I can't."

All around them, the night stilled. Not a breath of air moved. No barking dogs sounded out at a distance. No other cars drove down the dark road. Stars and moon shone down from a jet-black sky and seemed to wrap them both in a hungry silence.

"Why not?" he asked, though he knew the answer already.

"It wouldn't be right," she said, her gaze moving over his face like a touch.

"It feels right."

"I don't want to go, Jake."

He smiled. "Then stay."

She moved her hands on his chest, sliding her

palms over his tank top, her fingertips just brush-ing skin, leaving fire in their wake. He sucked in a gulp of air, tightened his arms around her waist and dipped his head closer toward hers.

She watched him advance, and he waited for her to pull away, to turn her head aside in an attempt to ward off his kiss. But she didn't. She only looked at him through clear blue eyes that seemed to look down deep inside him.

Her mouth was full and lush and only a breath away. He tasted it. Quickly, briefly, just a brush of his mouth on hers. She inhaled sharply, licked her lips, then cautiously moved into him.

Jake's heart in his throat now, he kissed her again, this time pouring all he felt, all he wished for, all he wanted into that one kiss. Her lips parted beneath his and his tongue swept into her heat, claiming her as he'd wanted to all summer.

She moaned and that tiny sound fed the flames within. Desire fisted in his throat, clamored in his blood and demanded more. Demanded everything.

His hands shifted, sliding up and down her spine, cupping her bottom, squeezing and then sliding back up as he tried to feel all of her. She moved against him and he wondered if she could feel how hard he was. Did she know what she was doing to him? Did she want it, too? Did she want him as badly as he wanted her?

Eagerly he lifted the hem of her tiny tank top

and slid his hands beneath the soft fabric. Her skin felt better than silk. Warm, smooth. Skimming his hands along her flesh, he reached higher, until he felt the undersides of her bare breasts.

She hissed in a breath and deepened their kiss, groaning and leaning into him. Her tongue entwined with his, their breaths mingling in a desperate dance of need.

And then his hands were full of her ripe breasts, his thumbs moving carefully across her hard nipples. She gasped at the sensation and jerked her head back to look at him.

Breath jittered in and out of her lungs as she watched him. He watched her, too, and saw passion glaze her eyes with every flick of his thumbs on her nipples.

"Donna," he managed to say on a choked groan, "I need—"

"Me, too, Jake" she admitted, "me, too."

She didn't do anything to stop him when he dropped his hands to the waistband of her shorts. Her hands ran up and down his arms in a silent plea for him to hurry.

His fingers fumbled with the snap and zipper of her denim cutoffs. He cursed under his breath and she laughed lightly, the music of it settling into him. Finally, though, he opened her shorts and in the next instant, he was sliding one hand beneath her flowered panties to find the heat he craved.

*Laughter died as she swayed and reached out
blindly for his shoulders. Her fingers dug into his
bare skin and he felt the imprint of each of her
short, neat nails digging into his flesh. But he
didn't care. Hardly noticed. All he could think was,
his dream had come true at last.*

Donna was his.

*At the first touch of his fingers at her center, she
shivered in his arms and gasped his name aloud.
"Jake, Jake, what...?"*

*He didn't know, either. He and his cousins had
talked plenty about times like these. But as much
as they liked to brag, none of them had ever gotten
further than unhooking the occasional bra.*

Tonight was different.

Tonight was special.

*He pushed his hand farther into her panties and
dipped one finger into her damp heat. The glory of
it filled him and urged him on. He stroked her, inside
and out, loving the slick feel of her on his hand.*

*She sucked in a gulp of air. Her eyes looked wild
and crazed. He kissed her and she kissed him
back—for one long, amazing minute.*

*Then she stopped suddenly, pulled his hand
from her and took a quick step back. Buttoning up
her shorts, adjusting her shirt, she shook her head.
"I can't do this. I can't let us do this."*

*"Donna." He took a step and winced with the
pain of trying to walk around a rock-hard erection.*

"I want to, really badly," she said, swallowing again and shaking her head more firmly, as if trying to convince herself of what she was saying. "Jake, you make me feel…I don't know…special. But we can't do this. What about Mac?"

"You want me, not Mac," he said shortly.

"Don't, Jake." She held up one hand to keep him at bay and hurried to the driver's side door of the car. "Just—don't. I'm sorry. I shouldn't have. I'm…sorry."

Then she jumped into the car, fired up the engine and with one last look of regret, drove past him, leaving him on the side of the road, wondering where the magic had gone.

Jake pulled in a long, shuddering breath and came back from the past with a jolt. Strange that one night so long ago could be so clear in his mind. So vivid that he could still feel both the need and Donna's rejection so completely.

He held on to the anger bubbling in the pit of his stomach as he looked down into eyes that were every bit as beautiful as they had been so long ago. Anger was a much safer emotion to cling to.

"You used me," he said tightly.

"What?"

"You came on to me," Jake accused, though even as he said it, he knew it was a lie. "Got yourself all fired up, then ran off to Mac."

"You seriously think I did that on *purpose?*"

"You were a tease, Donna."

"And you were a jerk," she snapped. "Just like you are now."

"You wanted *me*," he said, moving in on her with long, slow steps, even as she backed up.

At the end of the aisle, she came up short, glanced around as if mentally deciding whether or not to just bolt—then shifted her gaze to his. He saw her make the decision to stand her ground flash in her eyes and a part of him stood back and admired her for it.

"Yes, I wanted you," she said, pushing her hair back from her eyes with an impatient swipe of her hand. "I was young and stupid and when you touched me, I—"

"Burned?"

"Yes," she admitted with a sigh that released a pent-up breath. She wrapped her arms around her middle and hung on tightly. Her teeth tugged at her bottom lip again and Jake really hated the fact that the action could still have an effect on him. "I was *fifteen,* Jake. I'd never felt anything like that before and it scared me."

He nodded slowly and that small bit of patience cost him. "So you took what started between us and let Mac finish it."

"I was upset. Shaken." She lifted one hand to rub at a spot between her eyes. "When I left you on the road that night, I drove to the lake. Coop and

Sam were already gone. Mac saw something was bothering me. I didn't tell him," she said quickly, "about you and me, I mean. I just… I was crying and Mac was sweet. Gentle."

"And you and he—" God, he didn't want that image in his head. All the times he'd thought of that night. Of what might have been. All the times he'd waken up shaking, remembering her innocence, her eagerness, her breathless passion.

"I didn't mean for it to happen," she said, sighing. "It just did."

"Because Mac wasn't like me."

She lifted her chin and glared at him. "You're not going to let this go, are you?"

"Been trying to for fifteen years."

"Oh, please," she said with a strangled laugh. Pushing past him, she walked back to the counter and the stack of movies still waiting to be shelved. "You seriously don't expect me to believe you've given me a single thought over the years, do you?"

He caught up with her in a few long strides. Catching hold of her upper arm, he turned her around to look at him. "Can you tell me that you haven't thought of what happened between us that night? Can you look me in the eye and tell me it never haunts you? That you don't regret giving in to what was happening?"

Donna's breath caught in her chest and she swallowed hard past a knot of need that had suddenly erupted in the middle of her throat. Just one touch of Jake's hand and her skin was on fire.

"Is that what you need to hear?" she countered, without really answering his question at all. "Do you really need to believe that you were that unforgettable? We were *kids,* Jake."

"Uh-uh. We *stopped* being kids the minute we kissed."

His fingers tightened on her arm and as he bent his head toward hers, Donna knew she should do something. Anything. She couldn't get involved with Jake. Not now. Not when there was Eric to think about.

Besides, the bottom line was, Jake still made her scared of what she was feeling.

"There's unfinished business between us, Donna."

His voice, a deep, low rumble of sound seemed to roll over every last nerve in her body. Tingling sensations sprang into life within her. Heat pooled between her thighs and made her knees weak.

"Jake…"

"You smell the same," he whispered, dipping his head to the curve of her neck.

She held her breath and let it slide slowly from her lungs when his lips touched the base of her throat. A warning voice in her mind reminded her that they were at the video store. That there was a plate glass window opening onto Main Street. That *anyone* could come into the store at any moment.

But that logical, rational little voice was drowned out by the clamoring of her heartbeat and the desire already rocking her to her soul.

"Why did you have to come home?" she asked breathlessly.

"For this," he said, and covered her mouth with his.

Hunger.

Raw, undeniable hunger raged within her.

Every cell in her body leaped up and shouted in mindless joy.

He opened her mouth with his tongue and she met that intimate touch with abandon. Moving into him, she wrapped her arms around his neck and clung to him tightly. His mouth, more practiced now than on that long-ago night, brought her to the peak of want and pushed her over.

Again and again, his tongue plunged her depths and she gave herself up to the heat. Everything else faded away, the world, her job, her responsibilities and at once, she was that young girl again. Inexperienced and burning with a need she didn't understand.

Jake swept one hand down her spine and cupped her behind. She groaned into his mouth as he kneaded her flesh with strong, sure fingers. Then he shifted his grip, sliding his hand around to her front and through the fabric of her jeans, he cupped her aching heat. Applying steady pressure as he rubbed and stroked her, he brought her almost to the point of climax—and stopped.

Gasping for air, Donna swayed unsteadily and slapped one hand onto the counter to balance herself as she stared up at him. His dark eyes glittered with unassuaged hunger, with a need that dwarfed even her own.

"Jake, what're you…"

"Not here," he ground out, throwing one glance at the front windows and the empty sidewalk beyond the glass. "Not now."

Throat tight, heart racing, Donna struggled to find both air *and* her dignity.

"I want you," Jake told her, shoving both hands into his pockets as if he didn't quite trust himself not to make another grab for her. "And this time, I plan to *have* you."

A short, humorless laugh shot from her throat as Donna glared at him. "I was right. You haven't changed a bit. You're still Danger Man."

"Maybe I am," he agreed softly. "But you're not a fifteen-year-old virgin anymore, are you?"

"No, I'm not," she said, gathering the threads of self-control and holding tightly to them. "I'm an adult. A mother. With more to think about than feeding my own desires."

"Bull!!"

"I beg your pardon?" She tried for a dismissive sniff, but didn't quite pull it off.

He pulled one hand free of his pocket, tipped her chin up until their gazes met and looked at her squarely. "A minute ago, you were ready to ride me into a gallop right here on the floor."

She flushed, because damned if he wasn't right. Her brain had shut down and her body had taken over. Which is exactly why Jake had scared her so badly fifteen years ago. When she was with him, she didn't want to think about anything but being *with* him, *on* him.

"And soon," he promised, bending to give her a brief, hard kiss, "we're gonna take that ride together."

He brushed past her then, heading for the front door. Donna listened to his heavy boot steps across the gleaming tile floor and she turned just as he reached the doorway.

"Jake?"

He swiveled his head to look at her, one dark eyebrow lifting in silent question.

"Whatever's between you and me?" she said. "It doesn't give you an opening to Eric."

He frowned at her and shook his head. "You don't get it, Donna. We don't *need* an opening to Eric. He's a Lonergan. That makes him one of us. Family."

"His name is Eric *Barrett*."

"Doesn't make him any less a Lonergan, or us any less his family." Jake lifted one hand and touched his forehead in farewell. "I'll be seeing you, Donna."

Five

An hour later, Donna closed the shop early. If anyone in Coleville wanted to rent a movie for the night, they'd just have to make the thirty-mile drive to San Jose. No way was she going to stay in that shop surrounded by the fresh new memories of Jake holding her, kissing her.

Muttering darkly, she tossed her purse onto the front seat of her compact car, turned the key and fired up the engine. Putting the gearshift in reverse, she quickly backed out and drove for the house where she'd grown up, just a mile or so away.

It felt weird, being back home again. Nice, but weird. She'd been gone so long, had changed so much, that being back in her hometown felt almost…dreamlike.

Coleville seemed as though it had been standing still. The people she remembered were all older now, but the stores and the quiet, family-filled streets remained the same. Her hands fisted on the steering wheel as she drove slowly down Main Street, letting her gaze sweep the storefronts.

The tree-lined streets of Coleville were practically empty. No doubt, most everyone was more concerned with staying inside their air-conditioned homes than with shopping. And who could blame them. Summer was finally winding down, but it wasn't leaving without a fight. Heat waves danced across the road in front of her, wavering in the blistering sunlight like she supposed a mirage in the desert would.

But the heat within Donna had nothing to do with summer. It was all Jake's fault. She stopped at a red light and idly tapped her fingers against the steering wheel.

"Okay, so it's not *all* his fault," she muttered and closed her eyes against a fresh wave of heat that swept her up and down before settling to burn between her thighs.

"What is it about him that turns you into a walking hormone, anyway?" she asked herself, opening her eyes to glare at her reflection in the rearview mirror.

But she already knew the answer to that question. Even as a kid, Jake Lonergan was the epitome of a "bad boy." His hair was always a little too long, his jeans a little grubby, his T-shirts a little too tight and his eyes… "Oh, God, his eyes."

Her chin hit her chest. She was in bad trouble. And she couldn't afford to give in to her desires. Her wants. *Needs*. She had a fourteen-year-old son to think about. To protect.

Nodding grimly to herself, she turned left when the light turned green and headed down Lemon Street. Old growth trees leaned in toward each other over the street, creating a cool arch that dotted the road with lacy patterns of sunlight splashing through the leaves.

As she pulled into the driveway, she nodded at a neighbor, riding a lawn mower across his carefully tended lawn. She got out and heard not only the mower's loud engine but the sounds of barking dogs and laughing children, running through sprinklers across the street.

Good. Normalcy. This is good, she told herself, headed for the house. That little moment with Jake was *way* outside normal. But now things were back in place. *She* was back in control.

She could survive the rest of the summer. And then Jake would be gone. And hopefully, she'd never have to deal with him again. Yet even as that thought crept through her mind, Donna realized that she'd never be free of Jake entirely. Now that he knew about Mac's son, he'd expect—knowing Jake, *demand*—to be a part of the boy's life.

"Well fine," she said, opening the door and stepping into the blessed cool of her mother's living room. "That doesn't mean he has to be a part of *my* life."

"That you, honey?"

Her mother's voice sang out from the back of the house and Donna smiled. No matter the trouble she might be having with Jake, she'd done the right thing in coming home. She'd missed her mom over the years and being here with her now was important. To both of them.

"Yeah, it's me, Mom."

"Oh, good," Catherine said, bustling into the room, still primping her hair. "I wanted to talk to you before I left."

"Left?" Donna tossed her purse onto the blue-and-white, pin-striped couch. "Where're you going?"

Spinning around to face a mirror, Catherine ran the tip of her manicured finger over her eyebrows, each in turn, then grinned at her daughter. "Michael and I are going away for the weekend."

Yep, Donna thought, *good to be back home. Important for mom and I to have some time together.*

"The weekend?" she said aloud. "Together?"

Her mother frowned slightly. "I'm a big girl, Donna. I know what I'm doing."

"Fine, fine," Donna muttered, dropping onto the couch. "But I thought the three of us would go out to dinner tonight."

"That's sweet, honey," her mother said, coming across the room to stand in front of her. "But Michael and I have had these reservations at a bed and breakfast since before you moved home. I can't cancel on him."

"Of course not, but—" But what? She needed her mommy? How pitiful did that sound?

"You saw Jake today."

Her gaze snapped to her mom's. "How did you know that?"

"Eric told me."

"Eric?" Donna's mind raced. Sure, her son had seen Jake, but she hadn't introduced them. Of course, Eric was a smart kid. He knew his father's family lived in Coleville and there was enough of a resemblance between he and Jake that he'd probably noticed.

She blew out a breath. She'd wanted to talk to Eric about the Lonergans. But she'd been waiting for the right time. The perfect time.

Which, apparently was never going to appear now.

"How did he know that was Jake? I didn't introduce them or anything."

"He didn't know the man's name. But he described him, said he looked a lot like that old picture of Mac." Catherine inspected her manicure. "And once he got to the part about the guy having a ponytail and a Marine tattoo on his arm, I knew who the mystery man was."

Donna sighed. "You told him it was Jake."

"Sure did."

Groaning, she asked, "What else did he tell you about seeing him?"

"You mean besides the part about seeing you kissing Jake?"

"Oh, God." Donna dropped her head into her hands, remembering that fiery kiss and the hunger that had exploded between her and Jake. At the time, she hadn't given the storefront windows a moment's thought. *This,* she told herself, was what happened when you stopped thinking. "I'm an idiot."

"No, you're not," Catherine said, with a chuckle. "And Eric's not scarred forever."

"I've got to talk to him," Donna said, lifting her gaze to her mother's.

"He's not here."

"Not here?" Donna straightened up on the couch. "Where is he? Still with Jason?"

"No," Catherine said, perching on the arm of the couch and reaching for her daughter's hand. Giving it a pat, she said, "He came home a while ago, took his bike, then left again."

The concern in her mother's eyes worried Donna. A sinking sensation opened up inside her as she forced herself to ask, "Where'd he go?"

"To the Lonergan ranch."

"What?" She leaped up, pulled her hand from her mother's comforting grasp and started pacing. She only got a few hurried steps away before she whirled around and asked, "Why?"

Catherine gave her a long, steady look, one neatly arched eyebrow lifted in a silent question. "Why do you think? He wanted to talk to Jake."

"Oh," Donna grumbled, grabbing up her purse and heading for the front door, "this is just perfect. Perfect."

"Donna, don't overreact."

"I'm not overreacting," she countered, glancing back at her mom, "Eric's never seen me kissing a man. He's probably furious. And embarrassed." She paused for a breath. "Besides, I don't want him hanging around Jake. Nothing good can come of that."

"Interesting."

"What?"

"Oh," Catherine said, smoothing her gray skirt over her knees, "just that you don't seem to have any problems 'hanging around' Jake yourself. Funny that you're so anxious to keep Eric from him."

Sunlight slanted in through the wide front window and painted a slash of gold across the cozy living room. Fresh flowers filled a tall, rectangular vase sitting in the middle of the coffee table and the scent of lemon polish hovered in the air.

Donna drew on the familiarity, the warmth of the room to steady herself. How could she explain her feelings for Jake to her mother when she couldn't explain them to *herself?*

"The boy has a right to know *all* of his family," her mother said softly.

"I know that," Donna said. "And I want him to know and love Jeremiah. To learn more about his father. It's just that I don't quite trust Jake." There. She'd said it.

"Uh-huh," Catherine said, standing up and walking toward her, "are you sure it's not more that you don't trust yourself around Jake?"

Donna blinked up at her. "Huh?"

Catherine reached out and tucked a strand of Donna's hair behind her ear. "Honey, even when you were kids, there was something there between you and Jake. Anyone with half an eye could see it all over his face every time he looked at you."

"Oh, my…"

"In fact, the day you told your dad and me that you were pregnant, I fully expected to hear you say that Jake was the father."

"Mom," Donna hid her surprise behind a look of outrage. "Mac was my boyfriend."

"Oh, I know that, dear. But you and Jake had a connection that you and Mac simply didn't."

She couldn't believe what she was hearing. She remembered all too clearly seeing the shocked look of disappointment on both her parents' faces when they'd learned about her pregnancy. But she never guessed that her mother had been surprised at just who the father was.

But then, if she hadn't run away from Jake and everything he was making her feel that night, he *would* have been Eric's father. Still the point was, she *had* run. Because Jake wasn't the steady-boyfriend kind of guy. Heck, he still wasn't.

"I can't believe you're saying this to me," Donna said, slinging her purse strap over her shoulder. "Connections? With Jake? I was only fifteen."

"But you're not anymore," Catherine said softly. "And even back then, when you were just a girl, I think you knew what you wanted. You were simply too afraid to admit it."

"You're wrong, Mom," Donna said quietly. "I wasn't afraid to admit I wanted Jake. I just knew, even back then, that I *shouldn't* want him."

"People change," her mother reminded her.

"No, they don't," Donna said, giving her a sad smile. Then she reached out, gave her mom a quick hug, said, "Have a good time," then ran for her car.

Rock music pounded from the small radio on the workbench in the Lonergan barn. Usually Jake had music playing as background noise while he worked. *Usually,* when he was working, a bomb could go off under his feet and it wouldn't disrupt his concentration.

Of course, today was a little different.

Concentrating on a truck's carburetor wasn't easy when his lips were still burning and his blood was still pumping like thick, molten lava. He could still feel Donna's smooth, silky skin against his fingertips. Feel the heat of her through the fabric of her jeans.

And his groin was tight enough, hard enough, that he could hardly breathe with the wanting.

He slammed the wrench he was holding down onto the cluttered workbench and stared blankly at the pegboard in front of him. Probably shouldn't have gone to see Donna. He'd pried the lid off of emotions and sensations he'd been ignoring for years—and now he didn't know if he could keep on ignoring them.

Or even if he wanted to.

"Hey."

Jake spun around and looked into the face of a boy who was so much like Mac that for just one heart-stopping moment, he thought it *was* Mac. Come back from the dead to complain about Jake kissing *his* girlfriend?

He shook his head free of the nonsense and concentrated on Mac's son. "Hey, yourself."

The kid glanced around the barn as he walked slowly inside, pushing his ten-speed alongside him. Finally, though, he shifted dark eyes to Jake and looked at him for a long minute or two.

"I saw you kissing my mother."

Ah, damn it.

Jake scrubbed one hand against the back of his neck. Eric was only fourteen, but he'd come here like a man, not a little boy, so Jake would treat him like one.

"I've known your mom for a long time."

"Yeah, I know." The boy leaned his bike against the workbench and shoved both hands into the back pockets of his baggy jeans shorts. "You're my father's cousin."

"Yours, too," Jake said.

"I guess." Eric shrugged, looked away, then sharpened another glance at him. "So why'd you kiss her?"

Because he'd wanted her more than half his life? Because just standing in the same room with her was enough to make him as hard and horny as a teenager in the backseat of his daddy's car?

"That's between your mom and me."

The kid scowled. "I don't like it."

"Sorry to hear that," Jake said, "but maybe if you get to know me a little, you won't mind so much."

He considered that for a second or two. "Maybe.

But my mom doesn't want me coming out here to see you and the others."

"But you came anyway."

He shrugged. "To tell you I saw you guys."

This Jake understood. The need to protect. Defend.

"I'm sorry you saw us," he said, "but I'm not sorry I kissed her."

"You gonna do it again?"

"If she'll let me."

"She won't."

"We'll see." Jake folded his arms across his chest, braced his feet wide apart and watched the boy. His heart ached with the old blend of regret and guilt. For so many years, he'd tortured himself over Mac's death. Now, it was harder than ever. Not only had Mac missed living his *own* life, he'd missed knowing his *son.*

"So is my grandfather here?" Eric asked, pitching his voice to be heard over the radio.

"He's in the house. Along with your dad's other cousins."

"Yeah?" The boy looked back over his shoulder at the house. "Can I meet 'em?"

He wanted to just say *hell yeah.* But instead, he heard himself say, "You said your mother doesn't want you out here. So I'm guessing that means she doesn't know you're here now."

"Not exactly."

"Right." Jake nodded, hiding a smile. "C'mon. I'll take you inside so you can meet everybody. Then you can call your mom and tell her where you are."

"Okay," Eric said. "But I still don't like you kissing my mother."

"Understood."

Jake walked beside the kid, fighting the urge to drape one arm around those narrow, stiff shoulders and give him a hug. It wouldn't be welcome at the moment. The kid was too confused, and too pissed off at Jake.

But now that they'd finally connected, Jake was going to have to find a way to convince Donna to let them build on that connection.

He wouldn't lose this link to Mac.

Donna pulled into the driveway of the Lonergan ranch and drove all the way around to the back of the house. She was hoping to just collect Eric and make a quick escape. Maybe, if she was very lucky, Jake wasn't there at all.

As she came around the corner of the house, though, she sighed and parked her car. Not only were the Lonergans out in force, but it appeared they were having a little celebration in Eric's honor.

No way was she getting out fast now.

Already, Jeremiah was headed her way, a beaming smile creasing the lines on his face. In spite of everything, Donna was grinning as she climbed out of her car. She'd loved Mac's grandfather as much as he had. And she'd missed him over the years. She closed the car door behind her and stepped into a bear hug from Jeremiah.

"Donna, I'm so glad you came. Eric's a little overwhelmed I think, by all the new relatives. He could use his mom around." He pulled back, held her at arm's length and gave her a smile. "Can I talk you into a barbecued burger?"

She looked past Jeremiah's shoulder to the picnic table under the shade of the old tree in a corner of the ranch yard. Cooper, Sam, Jake and Eric were all hovering around the barbecue, while smoke lifted and twisted in a brief wind. Sam's fiancée, Maggie, was carrying a stack of plates from the house and another woman was standing guard with a fly swatter.

A ping of something sweet and sharp jolted through her system as she acknowledged that by all rights, Mac should have been in the middle of that family gathering. Instead, though, his son was there. Discovering cousins he'd never met. Enjoying the grandfather he'd only known for a couple of months.

Eric looked happy, surrounded by three men who looked so much like him. His eager gaze shot from one man to the next as he listened to them talk— no doubt they were telling him all sorts of stories about the father he'd never known. How could she tear him away? How could she prevent him from knowing his father the only way he ever would?

"Donna?" Jeremiah asked quietly. "Will you stay?"

She shifted her gaze to the lovely old man standing beside her and smiled. "I'll stay. For now."

Six

"Get your bike and put it in the trunk of the car," Donna told her son as she handed him the keys.

Eric's head drooped and he looked up at her from under a fall of dark hair. "Are you mad that I came out here without telling you?"

"You mean without *asking* me?" she corrected.

"Okay, yeah," he said with a shrug.

"No," she sighed. "I'm not mad. We'll talk about it later."

He lifted his head and gave her a grin. "Okay." Then he looked past her and called, "See ya, Jake."

Donna cringed a little as she heard the man come up behind her.

"See ya, kid."

His voice was deep and close. Very close. Then Eric was gone and she was alone with Jake. She felt his presence so clearly, it was as if he'd touched her. And if he did, she thought, she just might jump right out of her skin. Every nerve in her body was strained to the breaking point already. All it would take was the slightest nudge to push her over the edge.

Closing her eyes briefly, she tried to center herself with a little silent chanting. It didn't work. For the last two hours, she'd been surrounded by Lonergans. Eric had loved every minute of it, but Donna had been a little too tense to relax that much.

Sam's and Cooper's fiancées had been very nice and easy to talk to, but time and again, she'd been drawn into the conversations the men were having. Over barbecued burgers, the cousins and Jeremiah had told story after story about Mac—for Eric's benefit, she was sure. And her son had lapped it all up eagerly. In just a short amount of time, he'd learned more about his dad than he had in all his fourteen years. Donna had done her best to tell him about Mac, of course, but hearing him talked about with such love and affection by his family, made the father Eric had never known, real as he'd never been before.

But the memories dredged up had been hard for Donna to deal with.

She'd seen in Jake's eyes that he, too, was having more of a problem with the past than his cousins seemed to. More than once, their gazes had met across the table and pain, regret, had collided between them.

Now he was standing right beside her and damned if Donna could think of a thing to say.

"I'm glad you stayed," he said, breaking the silence between them.

She tore her gaze from her son, struggling to stuff the ten-speed into the trunk of her small car and looked at Jake. Instantly a flush of something hot and needy raced through her and it was all she could do to tamp it down deep. To help with that effort, she let her gaze slip past Jake to the house behind him. Lamplight filled nearly every window and the sounds of laughter drifted out the open back door.

The night was clear and cool and every star seemed to shine more brightly than usual. Or maybe that was just Donna's heightened senses playing games with her mind.

"I only stayed for Eric's sake."

"I know."

"It won't happen again."

"Never say never."

Donna blew out a breath. "Jake, this afternoon doesn't change anything. I still don't want Eric hanging around you."

"Why the hell not?" His brows drew together as he folded his muscular arms across his broad chest. Glaring down at her, he waited for an explanation.

She had one for him, but he wouldn't like it. He'd already proved that earlier. "Because," she started, "he's young, impressionable." She shot Eric a glance to make sure he was still out of earshot and satisfied, she turned back to Jake. "I saw the way he was watching you. Eyes all wide and interested every time you spoke. He's already halfway to idolizing you and I won't let that happen. You're too…"

"Let me guess," he practically growled. *"Dangerous?"*

"Well, yeah." She folded her own arms across her chest, right under her breasts. Instantly she realized her mistake, since the action pushed the tops of her breasts higher under the scoop necked tank top she wore and Jake was enjoying the view way too much. She let her arms drop to her sides again. Lowering her voice, she said, "Eric doesn't need to look up to you, Jake. He needs to find himself *by* himself. He needs to go to school, choose a career."

"And I didn't?" Jake said, clearly stunned.

"Please. You race motorcycles. That's not a career."

One dark eyebrow lifted. "Been keeping tabs on me?"

Yes, she thought, but that wasn't the point, was it? Besides, it wasn't as though she'd been following him through the years. She'd only done an Internet search on him the one time. And it had been enough.

Jake Lonergan, one of the articles had read, *rides his motorcycle like a man chasing death. The safe, careful moves seem never to occur to him. Instead, this competitor rides where no one else dares. He pushes his custom made bikes into speeds unheard of in racing circles. When Jake Lonergan enters a race, he rides to win—even at the cost of his own life.*

Those words rushed into her mind now and Donna just managed to squelch a shiver. Eric needed a male role model in his life. But he *didn't* need Jake.

Neither did she, no matter what her body might be telling her.

"Enough to know," she said quietly, gaze boring into his, "that you haven't changed any. You're still looking for the thrill. The rush. Just like when you were a kid, driving Jeremiah's truck like a crazy person. You compete in a dangerous business and even your competitors think you're crazy."

He frowned at her and straightened up to his full, very impressive height. "The racing is something I do because I like it."

"That's what concerns me," she muttered.

"But," he said, "it's not my whole life. I don't race all the time. I run my own business, too. *Jake's Choppers.* I design and build custom motorcycles for people with more money than style."

She hadn't known that. Probably could have found out, but she'd stopped reading about him the minute she'd reached that one specific article.

"That's nice, Jake, but—"

"And I fund a shelter for runaways in Long Beach."

"That's…" She paused and blinked up at him in stunned surprise. "You do?"

He nodded slowly, his gaze fixed on hers. "I'm also on the board of a number of companies I have holdings in."

"On the board…"

Donna couldn't quite grasp this. He stood in a wash of moonlight, looking like a modern day pirate, with his ponytail, scruffy jeans and dusty boots—not to mention the scowl on his face. Not exactly the mental image she carried of a regular businessman.

"And," he finished, his voice even lower, "my design company hosts a yearly challenge for new,

young engineers—giving them the chance to see their designs become reality."

"I didn't know," she said, and wasn't entirely sure about what to do with the information now that she had it. Did it change anything? Did any of this change Jake on a basic level? Just look at how he dressed. Still the rebel. Still pushing at the edge of an envelope only he could see. And he'd just admitted that he still liked to compete in dangerous races.

"You could have asked," he said tightly, his mouth a grim slash across his face.

She nodded. "Okay. Fine. I admit, there's more to you than I thought there was. But there's still the racing, Jake. Or, what one article called your habit of 'chasing death.'"

"Oh, for—" He scrubbed both hands across his face, glanced at Eric to make sure he was still fiddling with the bike and then asked Donna, "You *believed* that? One guy's opinion?"

"It sounded like you," she said. "And I don't want Eric to pick up on any of that."

"I'm not going to take him racing, Donna."

"No, you're not."

"But I won't stay away from him, either." His features softened. "He's a great kid."

Everything in her melted a little. The surest way to win a mother's heart was to compliment her child. "Yeah, he is."

"I wouldn't do anything to hurt him."

Emotion choked his voice and Donna knew it had cost him to reassure her. She blew out a breath she hadn't even been aware she was holding. "I know that, Jake. I really do."

"But?"

"But," she repeated, staring up into dark eyes that she knew would haunt her for the rest of her life, "that doesn't mean he wouldn't be hurt anyway."

"Mom," Eric called out, "the bike won't fit in your trunk."

"Put it in the back of Coop's car. That thing's big enough to carry a boat," Jake yelled back.

"Great," Eric said with enthusiasm, "can I drive?"

"No," Donna said instantly.

"Oh, man…"

Jake laughed. "Gotta give him points for trying."

"Jake—" Donna interrupted.

"Look, I'll drive him home, then you and I can finish this discussion tomorrow."

"I don't think that's a good idea."

"Over dinner?"

"Jake's coming for dinner?" Eric said as he passed by them on the way to Cooper's SUV. "Great. Can we have spaghetti?"

"Sounds good to me," Jake said, turning a questioning look on Donna.

She knew when she was beaten. At least for the moment. "Fine," she grumbled. "Spaghetti it is."

"Cool!" Eric's voice came to them from a distance.

"I'll bring the wine," Jake said and leaning down, planted a quick, hard kiss on her mouth before stalking across the yard to help Eric.

Donna stared after them for a second or two, trying to figure out just exactly when she'd lost control of the situation.

By the following afternoon, Jake was feeling like a kid getting ready for his first date. Stupid, he knew, but couldn't quite seem to squash the sensation. He'd actually enjoyed himself last night with Donna and Eric at the barbecue.

Until he'd noticed that every time one of the guys said Mac's name, Donna winced. And that small instinctive flinch fed the guilt that still grabbed at his insides like a fist, squeezing.

Shaking his head, he put the bottle of red wine into the bike's saddlebag, closed and locked the lid. Picking up his helmet off the workbench, he turned back to the bike and stopped short when he spotted Cooper in the barn's open doorway.

"What?"

"Always so damn friendly." Cooper chuckled and moseyed into the barn. Hands in the pockets of his black slacks, he moved slowly, like he always had.

"Aren't you afraid of getting dirt on those spiffy

black shoes of yours?" Jake asked, clutching the strap of the helmet.

Cooper ignored the question and asked one of his own. "Date with the lovely Donna, huh?"

"Not a date," Jake said, though in his mind, it was just that. "Just dinner. With her and Eric."

"Uh-huh." Cooper ran one fingertip across the top of the workbench, glanced at the accumulated dirt, then flicked it off. "So you're not still crazy about her."

Everything in him went cold and still. "What?"

"Come on, Jake. I'm not stupid. Wasn't stupid when we were kids, either." Cooper shrugged negligently and leaned back against the edge of the counter. "Mac never noticed. Hell, Mac never noticed much except the engines you guys were always working on. Always surprised me that you and Donna never hooked up."

Jake slammed the helmet down onto the motorcycle's black leather seat. "Back off, Coop."

"In a minute." Cooper tilted his head to one side and studied him. "I saw you with her last night, you know. Couldn't take your eyes off of her. I half expected her to burst into flames the way you were watching her."

"*This* is backing off?"

His cousin grinned. "Nope."

"We're done talking."

"Almost." Cooper pushed away from the bench

and took the few steps separating them until he was standing beside him. "I know what you're feeling, you know."

"Is that right?"

"You're still feeling guilty about Mac," Cooper said softly and the quiet words stabbed at him. "And that's what's keeping you from going after Donna like you should have fifteen years ago. I recognize the guilt in your eyes. Saw it in my own often enough."

Jake swallowed hard and tried to argue. But what could he say? He looked at Eric and felt the pangs of regret hammering away at his soul. There was nothing he could do to make up for what he *hadn't* done fifteen years ago and that remorse lived with him always.

"What's your point?"

"My point is, Jake," Cooper said, reaching out to lay one hand on his cousin's shoulders, "that you don't have anything to be guilty about. We were just kids. We didn't know Mac was in trouble. And besides," he added with an understanding smile, "*you're* the one who wanted to go into the lake after him, remember? It wasn't your fault. You should stop beating yourself up over it."

"Right," Jake muttered with a shake of his head. "Nobody's fault. It just happened. Mac died. We lived. Simple."

"Nothing about it was simple," Coop said,

letting him go and taking a step back. "But you don't have anything to be guilty about, either. If you still want Donna, go for it. You don't owe Mac anything."

But Jake knew better. Jake knew the real truth he'd managed to hide from everyone. Cooper had it right that Jake had been the one who'd wanted to go into the water after Mac. But it hadn't been because he'd been worried about his cousin.

No. He'd only been thinking of himself. He'd wanted to jump into the lake and drag Mac up before he broke Jake's record. It wasn't concern for Mac that had prompted his action. It was plain selfishness guiding him.

Just like it had been the night he and Donna had come so close to making love. He'd never been honest with Mac about his feelings for Donna. He'd never been man enough to admit that he was in love with his cousin's girlfriend.

And that guilt was something he couldn't bring himself to tell anyone.

"Let it go, Coop. Okay?"

"I'm just saying…"

"I get it. Now, let it go."

"All right," Cooper said, already moving toward the door. He stopped in a slice of moonlight, turned and looked back at Jake. "But you should know that last night, I also noticed the way Donna was looking at *you*. And if you let her get away this time, then you're a moron."

"Dinner was good."

Donna looked up as Jake took the wet dish and slowly dried it. "Thanks, but spaghetti? Pretty hard to screw it up."

He grinned. "I've managed it."

She felt a smile building inside her and fought it back down. She'd had a good time with him and Eric. Too good. With her mom out of town, it had been just the three of them for dinner and a couple of times during the meal, they'd almost felt like a family. With Eric talking about his friend Jason and the skateboarding park on the outside of town. Then Jake had entertained them both with stories of all the countries he'd been to—of the things he'd seen.

A part of Donna envied him for his adventures. Even though she wouldn't have traded the time she'd had with Eric for anything, there were places she still wanted to go. Things she'd always planned to do.

"You're thinking," he said, his voice gruff and rumbly along her spine.

"Sorry," she said, forcing a smile that didn't feel quite real. Then she reached for a comfortable lie. "Just wondering if Eric remembered to take his...toothbrush with him to Jason's house."

And of course, she was wishing she'd told Eric no when his best friend had called to invite him over to spend the night. If she'd just crushed his plans, he'd still be here to chaperone her and Jake.

Pitiful, she thought. Wanting to use her fourteen-year-old son to keep her own hormones in check.

"He got everything," Jake said, taking the next dish from her after she'd washed it. "And is that what you were really thinking?"

"No," she admitted with a sigh. Pulling the plug in the sink, she stared, fascinated, as the water whirlpooled down the drain. "I was thinking about all the places you talked about at dinner. Spain. Italy. Switzerland." She swiveled her head and looked up at him. "I've always wanted to see the world."

"There's nothing stopping you."

She laughed shortly. "Right. Just Eric. And my job. And my mom. And—"

"Okay, it wouldn't be easy, but if you want something, you should do all you can to get it."

His tone, more than his words, reached her on some deep, elemental level and left her shaking inside. Slowly she lifted her gaze to his and felt a hard jolt when she read the hot flash of desire written in those dark depths.

"Jake…"

He tossed the dish towel down onto the counter and moved to capture her. He braced one hand on either side of her and leaned in. Donna pulled in a shaky breath and let it slide slowly from her lungs.

Her mother's cozy kitchen felt familiar, warm. The scent of dinner still hung in the air and the sizzle of something more erupted between them.

"Donna, there's something here. Between us. Always has been."

"I'm not saying there isn't." She should be, she just wouldn't. Couldn't. Impossible to lie to him about something like that when he could probably see the flames flickering in her eyes. "I'm only saying that we shouldn't—"

"Why not?"

"Because of Eric and—"

"Eric's not here."

"No, he's not." *Why* had she let him leave? Stupid, stupid. "But he will be tomorrow. And the day after that and the day after that."

"And you're not allowed to have a life until he's grown and out on his own?"

That sounded wrong. Even though it was exactly the way she'd been living until Jake had come back to town. She'd concentrated solely on Eric for so long, she barely remembered having any dreams that didn't center on her son. He was the most important person in her life, but she knew that if she didn't eventually find a life of her own, she'd have nothing when Eric grew up and moved on. Still…

"No, but any decision I make affects him."

He moved his hands closer to her sides. Close

enough that she could almost feel his touch. Close enough that she wanted to move into him so she *would* feel his hands on her. Oh, boy.

"Agreed," he said, dipping his head until his mouth was just a breath away from hers. "But at the moment, it's just the two of us."

"Jake," she said, closing her eyes because she couldn't trust herself to turn away if she was looking at him. She sucked in a gulp of air. "Please don't do this."

He lifted one hand and smoothed his fingers over the curve of her breast and even through the fabric of her pale blue T-shirt, she felt the heat of him. She blew out that breath and hoped wildly that she'd be able to draw another at some point.

"You really want me to leave?"

"No," she admitted, grabbing his hand and holding it tightly. She chewed frantically at her bottom lip. "So you really should."

He stepped back from her and nodded. "Okay, if that's what you really want, I will. On one condition."

"You just can't take no for an answer, can you?"

He grinned. "No."

Donna sighed. "Fine. What's the condition."

"Come for a moonlight ride with me."

She hadn't been expecting that. "On your motorcycle?"

"Yep. Now."

"Oh, I don't know," she said, shaking her head,

"I already told Eric he couldn't ride that motorcycle of yours and—"

"I won't take Eric on it," he said, holding one hand out to her, "but I want to take *you*."

Dumb, Donna. Really, really dumb. Silently she laid her hand in his and her breath caught when he smiled at her. She'd probably regret this in the morning, Donna thought, but right now, there was nothing she wanted more than to be sitting behind Jake on a motorcycle headed into the night.

Seven

Darkness swirled around them as the wind rushed past the motorcycle. Jake concentrated on the road ahead, but another part of his brain was focused on the fact that Donna was sitting right behind him, pressed up close. Her thighs rested along his, her arms were wrapped tight around his middle and he could have sworn he felt the heat of her hard, pebbled nipples burning into his back.

His groin ached and his blood pumped thickly through his veins. The familiar roads all looked somehow different to him tonight, with Donna by him. The summer air was rich and sweet with the heavy scent of jasmine and the road was empty enough that it felt as though they had the night to themselves.

All his life, Jake had loved speed. Fast cars, fast bikes. He made his living building custom choppers for those with enough money to indulge themselves—but *lived* to race. To chase the edge of danger. There was nothing quite like feeling the world race past you. The adrenaline rush that came from cheating death was more powerful than anything he'd ever felt.

Until tonight.

The feel of Donna's arms tightening around his waist, her breath warm against the back of his neck, the heat of her body pressing into his—*nothing* compared to that. Nothing even came close.

Surprisingly enough, he wasn't interested in speed tonight. He wanted to slow down. For the first time in his life, Jake wanted to throttle back on the bike's powerful engine. Yet he knew, that even as he wished for *more* time, the few moments he had with her were quickly slipping past.

"Where're we going?" she asked, her mouth close to his ear, her voice barely rising above the roar of the engine.

"Does it matter?" he shouted back, fists tightening around the handlebar grips.

"No." She laid her head against his shoulder and everything inside him lit up like the sky at a Fourth of July picnic.

Jake clenched his teeth and fought the rising tide of need making his body ache and thrum with pent-up desire. There was only one place he wanted to take her. *Had* to take her.

He didn't need streetlights to guide the way. He remembered these back roads so well, he could have found the grove blindfolded. Which he might as well have been. The quarter moon was just a slice of light in a dark sky filled with the distant flicker of stars. Blackness stretched out on either side of the road—broken only by the occasional splash of light coming from a farmhouse window.

Jake turned right down a rocky path and he felt Donna stiffen on the seat beside him. She recognized the road, too. But she didn't ask him to stop. Didn't tell him to go back. He was grateful, because he wasn't sure he'd be able to do as she asked.

In the distance, a darker shadow crouched in the black night and Jake headed right for it. This small grove of scrub oaks held a special place in his memory. It was the place he dreamed of, when he allowed himself to. It filled his mind with the scents and sounds of that last summer. Of that one hot, moonlit night when he and Donna had almost—

He parked the bike at the edge of the trees and shut off the engine. In the sudden silence, he sat still, feet braced on the grass at either side of the bike, holding them both upright.

Crickets chirped and a slight breeze drifted

through the trees, rattling leaves until they sounded like hushed whispers from a fascinated crowd. He put down the kickstand and waited for Donna to climb off the bike before he moved. She walked directly toward the nearest tree and stretched out one hand to touch the knobby bark. She pulled her fingers back fast, as if she'd been burned. Then she turned to look at him.

His eyes, long adjusted to the darkness, fixed on her features and he read the strain—and the memories—in her eyes.

"Why'd you bring me here, Jake?"

He scowled slightly, shoved both hands into his pockets and walked toward her, his boot steps crunching on the dirt and grass beneath his feet. Now that they were there, at the spot where he'd imagined her so many times, he didn't really know what to say.

How the hell could he admit to her that the time they'd spent together here, in this shadowed grove of trees, was the best night of his life? How pitiful did that sound? A grown man holding on to a memory of a seventeen-year-old boy's first love?

No. Couldn't tell her that. Couldn't tell her that no woman since her had meant a damn to him. Couldn't even admit to himself that desire had never felt as thick and hot and *necessary* as it had the first time he'd touched her.

Instead he said, "Seemed like a good idea at the time."

"It's not," she said simply, wrapping both arms around her middle and hanging on. Her eyes clouded and she bit at her bottom lip. "It's…painful."

His head whipped up and his gaze pinned her. "Why painful?" he asked harshly, his voice straining over the words. "Because of what we almost did? Or because we didn't do it?"

She blew out a long, shuddering breath. "Both."

Something hitched in his chest and Jake grabbed a lungful of air. He took one long step, grabbed her arm and pulled her close. Her head fell back and her gaze met his. He saw the moon and the stars reflected in her eyes and a pulsing rush of desire swept through him.

"There was no pain between us that night, Donna," he muttered thickly.

"It was a mistake then," Donna whispered, licking dry lips and struggling for air, "and it would be a mistake now."

His grip on her arm gentled, but his hold on her was no less firm. Taking hold of her other arm, he rubbed her skin with his thumbs, relishing the feel beneath his hands again. Shaking his head, he said softly, "The only mistake that night was when you ran away from me."

She swallowed hard, tossed her hair back out of her face and asked, "I told you why I ran. I was fifteen and *scared*. Scared of you. Of what you made me feel."

"Do you think I *wasn't?*" He laughed shortly, no humor in the sound. "I wasn't that much older than you, you know. And I'd never felt before what I did that night."

Her eyes closed and a tired sigh slipped from her. "Why are you doing this, Jake? It's been fifteen years. Why now?"

His gaze moved over her features and in his heart, she looked exactly as she had on that long-ago night. Her eyes then had shone with innocence and a need she hadn't understood. He'd been seventeen and not much more experienced than she. But he had known that he wanted her. Needed her.

And that, apparently, hadn't changed.

"Because just being near you brings it all back. I've thought about you," he admitted. "Over the years, you stayed with me. Always at the edges of my mind. Always reminding me of what we almost had. What we almost found."

"Jake…"

"Tell me you haven't thought of me," he demanded, locking his gaze with hers, silently daring her to look away. His hands on her upper arms tightened. "Tell me honestly that you've never once regretted running away that night— and I'll take you home now and never mention this again."

She slumped in his grip, but didn't look away from him. Seconds ticked past and all he heard was the sigh of the wind and the song of the crickets. His own heartbeat crashed in his chest and he felt flames licking at his insides.

Finally when Jake thought his will would snap, she spoke.

"Regret doesn't change anything."

"That's not an answer."

"You know the answer, Jake," she said, staring deeply into his eyes. "But it still changes nothing."

"We can change it."

"Can we?" she asked, shaking her head. "*Should* we?"

"We're not kids anymore, Donna." His gaze moved over her, hungry. "There's no reason to run. No reason to not feel what we want to feel."

She laughed shortly. "Of course there are reasons," she said on a sigh. "Too many to count."

"They don't matter," he said, watching emotions flit across her eyes too quickly for him to identify.

"Don't they?"

"I wanted you then," he said, his voice scraping against his throat. "And I want you now. That's all that matters tonight."

Briefly she dropped her forehead to his chest, then lifted her head to look at him again. "Even then, Jake, you were a hard man to resist."

"You managed," he said, hiding the sting of the truth behind a small smile.

"It wasn't easy," she admitted, "but I was so scared…"

"Yeah. You said that before. I scared you so bad you ran to Mac."

She stiffened slightly. "Mac was sweet. Gentle. Kind."

"Everything I wasn't?" That stung, too, but he wouldn't let her know.

"Don't, Jake. Don't do this." She shook her head, and her hair swung in a soft arc.

"You wanted *me,*" he said, "not Mac."

Her eyes closed as she nodded. "I did want you," she admitted. "But I *wanted* to want Mac."

"Did it work?" he demanded as the wind soughed over them both like a blessing. "When you were with him, did you see *him?* Or were you seeing *me?* Feeling *me?*"

She looked up into his eyes and he saw truth shining in her eyes. "Do you really need to hear this?"

"After fifteen years, I think I deserve to hear it."

"Fine. It was you, Jake. It was *always* you."

"So you do remember what we felt."

"How could I forget?"

That was all he needed to know. He pulled her closer, lifting her up until she stood on her toes and her mouth was just a breath away from his. Staring down into her eyes, he bent his head closer, closer, lingering over the sweet rush of expectation.

Then his mouth closed on hers and the years fell away. He sighed and gave himself up to the rush of heat clamoring within.

Donna groaned, her lips parting beneath Jake's to welcome his sweet invasion. Her pulse jumped and skittered, her heartbeat jolted into a frenetic beat and her tongue tangled with his in a desperate, breathless dance of need. Not since that one night so long ago had she felt so many different emotions clattering inside her.

Her body came alive and desires she'd long suppressed erupted with a vengeance. Every nerve ending felt as though it were on fire. Every touch of his hands on her arms, then her back and down to the curve of her behind, felt as though his skin was flame and she was dry tinder.

He pulled her tighter against him and she wrapped her arms around his neck and held on, pressing herself as close to him as she could possibly get. Her nipples ached and her stomach spun with the wash of emotion lancing through her.

His big hands cupped her bottom and lifted, holding her tightly to the hard press of his groin. Heat flashed and her core tingled into awareness. She lifted her legs, wrapped them around his middle and moved on him, swiveling her hips even as her tongue tasted more of him and gave more of herself.

It had been years since she'd known this desperation. Years since she'd allowed herself to even dwell on the magic she'd once felt in Jake's arms. It was only in her dreams when her iron will gave way and the memories she'd suppressed came to life. Only then, in the middle of a lonely night, did she allow herself to remember and to wonder.

Donna had spent the last fifteen years trying to bury her own needs in favor of raising her son. Eric was what mattered. He deserved her attention. Her focus. And yet, she thought now, as Jake's hands brought her eager body to life, couldn't she allow herself one night? A few hours when she belonged only to herself and her own desires?

When she was a girl, she'd been too terrified of what she was feeling to let it happen. Now, the thought of *not* experiencing what Jake had to offer was the only thing scaring her.

He skimmed one hand around to slide between their bodies and her brain shut off. She didn't want to think. She only wanted to feel. Just for this one moment in time, she wanted what she'd never had. And she'd worry about the consequences later.

His thumb and forefinger flicked open the button at her waistband and then as she shifted in his grasp, making room, he tugged the zipper of her jeans down. Donna broke their kiss, threw her head back and stared at the starlit sky as he dipped his fingers down, beneath her panties, to skim the heat at her center.

Her legs flexed around his middle and she hissed in a breath as she tried to help him. Tried to make room for his touch.

"Can't reach you. Can't...feel you," he muttered, bending his head to rake the edges of his teeth along her throat.

Frustration rattled her. She didn't want to move out of his arms, but she needed to feel his hands on her. She was through pretending. Through lying to herself. She'd always wanted Jake's touch and tonight, she would have it. At last.

"Touch me, Jake," she sighed, her muscles quivering with the banked need within. "Have to touch me, now."

He growled, low in his throat, grabbed her waist, swung her off of him and stood her up against a tree. The rough bark bit into her back through the fabric of her T-shirt, but she didn't care. All she cared about was the look in his eyes as he worked her jeans and panties down the length of her legs. She kicked off her shoes and stepped out of her clothes, enjoying the kiss of the wind on her bare, heated skin.

She trembled, her knees weak, blood pumping. Her gaze locked on Jake's eyes and in those dark depths, she read the same hunger enveloping her. Seeing that desire etched into his features was like laying a match to the fuse on a stick of dynamite.

But in an instant, his expression changed. Darkened.

"What?" she asked, barely able to form the single word.

He looked like he wanted to kick something. "I don't have anything with me." At her blank look, he ground out, *"Condoms."*

Donna chuckled. "Big, bad Jake Lonergan doesn't carry condoms in his wallet anymore?"

He scrubbed one hand across his face. "I'm not a randy kid looking to get lucky anymore."

She pulled in a shaky breath. Here was her chance. To stop this before it went any further. But she wasn't going to do that and she knew it. "You're about to get really lucky," she said, her voice low, husky with the need clutching at her throat.

"Yeah?"

"Yeah. If you swear to me you're healthy," she said, holding up one finger to point at him.

"I am," he said, clearly affronted that she would even think he'd touch her if he weren't.

"Me, too," she said, then added, *"and,* I'm on the pill."

"That might be the best news I've ever heard," he said softly, moving in closer.

"I feel just the same way," she said, licking dry lips in eager anticipation.

"You're beautiful," he whispered. "Even more beautiful than you were then."

Donna *felt* beautiful. Naked in the moonlight, she read his hunger for her in his eyes and basked in the knowledge that this man wanted her as desperately as she did him.

She struggled for air as he stripped off his T-shirt, exposing his broad, muscled chest to her avid gaze. She reached out one hand and skimmed her fingertips across his skin and smiled when he shuddered. Then he was pulling off her T-shirt and tossing it to the ground with his. She stood naked, under the moon, with the breath of wind caressing her flesh. A swirl of something powerful and sexy rushed through her and Donna felt the thrill of the forbidden rise up within.

His fingers worked the buttons of his fly and she stepped up to him, walking into his arms as if it was where she'd always belonged. She jumped up and he caught her as she linked her legs around his waist and wrapped her arms around his neck. Her breasts pressed to his chest, she felt sharp blasts of heat jolting through her system and when his hands came down hard onto her hips, she knew he felt it, too.

Their gazes locked, he reached between their bodies to cup her heat. Donna hissed in a breath and held it as his long, talented fingers caressed her most sensitized flesh. Once, twice, he smoothed his fingertips across her heat and then finally, finally, slipped those fingers deep within her. Donna gulped for air and rode his hand with an urgency she'd never experienced before. She kept her eyes wide open, staring into his gaze as he pushed her higher, higher up the ragged slope of anticipation.

She trembled, shuddered and clutched at his shoulders as the first wave of something amazing shook her to her bones. Calling out his name, she rocked her hips, seeking, seeking… "Please, Jake," she groaned, voice tight, pleading. "Please…"

"Come for me, baby," he crooned, gaze never leaving her face. "Let go and fall. I'll catch you."

Unable to hold back any longer, she did what he urged and gave herself up to the brightly colored lights flooding her vision. Her body quaked in unbelievable pleasure as his strong arms held her tightly, safely. She relaxed and let herself be what she'd always wanted to be.

Wild.

With Jake.

And before the last of the tremors had claimed her, he pulled his hand free, held her hips tight and pushed his hard, solid length inside her. Donna gasped at the full, tight fit of him within. He was more than she'd imagined. More than she'd expected.

"You feel so good," he whispered, burying his face in the curve of her neck.

"And you feel…" She paused, looking for just the right word and coming up empty. Finally she simply said, "…*right*. You feel *right*."

He smiled, then that smile dissolved into a

whirlpool of desire. He held her tightly, then lifted her hips, sliding her off his shaft only to slam her back down again. He guided the rhythm between them. He fed the fires. He stoked the flames. He was all. He filled her body, her mind and her soul.

Nothing beyond this grove of trees, this exquisite sensation of being linked with him, existed. They were caught in a world apart. A world where only the two of them belonged. She wouldn't even let herself think about that world ending with the first rays of sunshine.

In the moonlight, sheltered beneath the gnarled oaks, they found the magic they'd lost so long ago.

And when their bodies climaxed, the explosion shocked them both and left them clinging together like shipwrecked survivors—not sure what to do next.

An hour or two later, Jake lay stretched out on the warm grass with Donna lying bonelessly atop him. They'd taken each other over and over again until now neither of them had the strength to sit up. He couldn't remember a better night in his life.

He ran one hand along her spine and smiled to himself when she moaned. She was more than he'd dreamed. More than he'd ever hoped. And yet, she still wasn't his. He felt it. He knew she'd shared his passion. But when this night was over, she'd run again.

Not to Mac.

But she'd run anyway.

"What're you thinking?"

He shifted a look at her as she folded her hands on his chest and propped her chin on them. "What makes you think I'm thinking at all?"

"Your brow's all scrunched up."

"It is?" He lifted one hand to check, then made a conscious effort to relax his forehead.

"So, do you want to tell me?"

"Not really," he said, knowing that if he brought up the idea of her running—she'd go. And he wasn't ready to give her up just yet. He'd waited a long time for this night.

Nodding, she said, "Then I'll tell you what I'm thinking instead."

"All right."

"I'm thinking that as wonderful as this was," she said, her voice filled with a regret he knew was real, "it can't happen again."

Jake laughed shortly and she frowned. "What?"

"*This* is what I was thinking," he said, giving her bare behind a small slap. "That soon enough you'd be running away again."

She pushed herself up until she was sitting, straddling him and looking down into his eyes. "I'm not running. I'm just saying—"

"That I'm still not good enough?" he managed to say.

"That's not it and you know it."

She tried to slide off of him, but he held her still with one strong hand on each of her thighs. "Then why?"

"Because I can't just do whatever I want to do," she said, covering his hands with her own. "I have a *son*. I have to think of *him*."

"This has nothing to do with Eric."

"Of course it does. I'm his mother. My focus should be on him, not on—"

"—sex?" he finished for her, sliding one hand to the core of her heat. His thumb stroked the bud of flesh at the heart of her and she sucked in air like a drowning woman.

"That's not fair."

He laughed again. "Who's interested in playing fair?"

"Damn it, Jake…" She twisted her hips, rocking into his touch, biting down on her bottom lip and shivering. "This doesn't solve anything."

"Maybe it doesn't have to," he said, moving his hands to her hips again. He eased her up, then guided her down onto his length.

She took him inside her, one slow inch at a time, driving them both insane with want, extending the pleasure until it was a raging force rising up between them. Finally he was embedded fully within her and she gulped for air as she swiveled her hips.

"Donna…" His fingers dug into her hips. He

looked up at her and through the passion glazing his eyes, he watched her stretch her hands high over her head.

He reached up, covering her breasts with his palms and his breath strangled in his throat as she covered his hands with her own, holding him to her. She moved on him, throwing her head back, riding him with abandon, giving herself over to the sensations coursing through them.

Jake couldn't take his gaze from her. His body reacted, rocking into hers, moving into the rhythm that already felt familiar between them. Moonlight spilled over her, gilding her in a pale wash of light that made her look like a dream.

But as she took him to the edge, then flew over the precipice with him, he knew she was all too real. And that if he allowed himself, he could love her.

Then losing her again would kill him.

Eight

"What're you doing here?" Jake asked three days later as Eric strolled slowly into the Lonergan barn.

The tall boy shrugged and it looked as if his whole body moved with the motion. "Nothing," he said, his gaze shifting over the workbench, landing on the tools neatly laid out atop it. "Just rode over to say hi."

"Does your mom know?"

"I left her a note."

Jake nodded. "A note she won't find till she gets home from work."

"Well, yeah." Eric gave him a half smile that was so much his father it stole Jake's breath. "She doesn't want me hanging around you," the boy admitted, now walking up to the motorcycle, gleaming in a splash of sunlight.

He ran one finger across the black and chrome gas tank. "She's worried that you're a bad influence."

"She said that?" Jake's teeth clenched. Damn it, it was one thing for her to voice her worries to his face. It was something else for her to turn Mac's son against him.

Eric swung his hair back out of his eyes. "I heard her tell my grandma."

Perfect.

A bad influence.

Seems nothing had been settled between them after all. Three days since he and Donna had had their long-promised night in the grove. Three days and not a damn word from her. He'd called her house, left messages, spoken to her mother, and nothing.

It was as if the woman he'd been with that night had disappeared into his memory as surely as she had fifteen years ago.

Watching his young cousin, Jake tried to hold on to the cold knot of disappointment lodged in his chest. But it wasn't easy. Hell, he could understand what Donna was thinking. If he had a son, he wouldn't want the kid emulating his lifestyle, either.

But then Jake had never had a reason to take a different path in his life. Except for his grandfather and his cousins, he had no family. No ties. No one depending on him for anything. Why the hell shouldn't he go out and enter races? Why shouldn't he take chances that men with families refused to?

Frowning to himself, he shoved those and other thoughts aside and focused on the kid now squatting for a closer look at the bike. "You like working on engines?"

Eric glanced up at him and grinned again. It was going to take a while to get used to seeing Mac's smile on this kid's face.

"Yeah, but I don't know enough to really do anything much."

"I could teach you," he blurted, then inwardly winced, knowing already what Donna would have to say about that.

"Really?" The kid lit up like a lightbulb. "That would be great." Then he frowned. "Mom probably won't let me, though."

"I'll fix it with your mom." Brave words, he thought, already mentally planning for the confrontation with Donna.

"Cool."

Jake nodded and leaned back against the workbench, the edge of the wood biting into the small of his back. Folding his arms across his chest, he said, "But first, go into the house, call the video store and tell your mom where you are."

Eric stood up and shoved both hands into his

jeans pockets, nearly pulling the baggy pants right off his narrow hips. "She'll tell me to go home."

"I'll talk to her after you."

"Okay."

"That's two dollars for a five-day rental," Donna said, taking the money from her customer and sliding the DVD into a rental case.

As the woman left with her movie, the phone rang and Donna snatched it up, keeping her eye on a couple of teenagers in the horror section. "Hello, Movie Time."

"Hi, Mom," Eric said and kept talking, words tumbling into each other, "just wanted to let you know I'm at Grandpa's and Jake's letting me help him work on his bike."

Her stomach dropped. "Eric…"

"Jake wants to talk to you, bye, Mom," her son said, quickly handing off the phone.

"Hi."

"Hi." She closed her eyes, temporarily forgetting about possible shoplifters in the horror section. Jake's deep voice reverberated inside her, setting up a series of earthquakelike jolts that had her reaching for the nearby stool. Dropping onto it, Donna opened her eyes again and focused on the teenagers even while her brain was doing a happy dance back to the events of three days ago.

Three whole days and her body was still alive and humming. She couldn't even remember how many times they'd come together over the few hours they'd spent in the grove. But she could remember every buzz of excitement, every burning need, every questing touch and taste.

The vivid memories had kept her from sleeping for the last couple of nights. And she didn't know how much more of it she could take. But she'd done what she thought best. She'd kept her distance from Jake, realizing that being alone with him again would only make his inevitable leaving that much harder to take.

She didn't have a future with Jake.

Didn't *want* a future with Jake.

He was everything she'd spent most of her life avoiding. Life on the edge. No commitments. No rules. No obligations.

Even as a girl, she'd known what she wanted. Family. A home.

And Jake was *not* the man to be interested in those things.

So what good would it do her to let herself care? To let herself enjoy being in his arms? To come to count on his kiss?

Oh, boy, she really missed his kisses.

"Donna?" he said, deep voice low, concerned. "You there?"

"Yes, Jake," she said, frowning as she noticed

one of the teenage boys slipping a movie under his shirt. "But I can't talk now."

"Fine. Eric's going to be here for a few hours. Why don't you come over after work?"

The boys were headed for the front door now and Donna was already standing up to head them off. "Fine. Okay. But we're going to be talking about this. Goodbye, Jake."

She slammed the phone down, stepped out from behind the counter and stood directly in front of the boys. They wouldn't meet her gaze. Holding out one hand, she said softly, "Let's have it."

Grumbling guiltily, the taller boy pulled the movie out from under his shirt and cringed a little. "You gonna call the cops?"

"Nope," she said, taking both their arms and leading them toward the counter. "I'm going to call your *mothers*."

"Oh, man…"

"You idiot," his friend said, reaching across Donna to punch his pal in the arm. "I told you not to take it."

Donna shook her head. They were a little younger than Eric, so she didn't want to call the police. No doubt they were good kids just trying to get away with something. Now they'd learn that everything had consequences. Something *she'd* learned the hard way, at fifteen.

Guiding them to the phone, she picked up the

receiver and handed it to the first boy. "Dial," she said and tried not to smile as the kid groaned and punched in a number.

When she arrived at the Lonergan ranch two hours later, the afternoon sun was casting long shadows across the yard and a light was burning in the barn. She stepped out of her car and was instantly greeted by the sound of male laughter.

Donna sighed. How could she ever hope to keep Eric away from his cousins? His family? He so clearly needed to be around these guys. So obviously enjoyed being a part of a bigger family.

As she walked toward the barn, she asked herself some hard questions and tried to answer herself honestly. Was she trying to keep Eric from the Lonergans for his sake, or for her own? Was she really worried about Jake and the others influencing Eric? Or did she simply not trust herself around Jake?

Was she being protective of her son?

Or was this more about protecting herself?

Maybe, she acknowledged, it was a little of both. Maybe if she simply accepted the fact that the Lonergans were now going to be a permanent part of Eric's life, she would be able to find a way to deal with it. To deal with seeing Jake and the others.

She kicked a pebble across the driveway, her

sneaker shooting a mini cloud of dust up into the air. Her son's laughter rolled out of the open barn doors to greet her and she smiled, despite the turmoil within. No matter what else she was feeling about Jake and the rest of the Lonergans, they'd accepted Eric wholeheartedly and she knew how much that meant to her son.

Cooper was telling a story when she stepped into the barn and she paused in the doorway so she wouldn't interrupt him.

"So, Jake," Cooper said to Eric with a grin, "he decides that Grandma's washing machine is running too slow. He tells your dad that while Grandma and Jeremiah are out to dinner, they should 'fix it.'"

"Don't listen to him, Eric," Jake said, giving Cooper a friendly shove. "He's all talk."

"Believe every word," Sam said, tossing Jake a beer.

"So what happened?" Eric asked, gaze fixed on Cooper.

"Your dad and Jake tore that old machine apart and had it put back together again by the time Grandma and Jeremiah got back."

"So they did it?" Eric asked. "They fixed the washing machine?"

"Oh, yeah, they fixed it all right," Sam said, laughing.

"It was Mac's fault," Jake piped up, taking a

long drink of his beer. "I told him he had the gears greased too much."

"Uh-huh," Cooper said with a sneer. Then turning back to Eric, he said, "Next morning, Grandma does a load of wash…"

Sam snorted a laugh and shook his head.

"The washing machine runs so fast, it jerks away from the wall, dances halfway across the kitchen, tears the hose out from the wall and water's shooting up like an upside down waterfall."

Eric laughed, looking from Cooper to Jake to Sam and back again.

"Grandma's screaming, Jeremiah's shouting, water's pouring all over the floor and the dog's trying to swim into the living room." Cooper, laughing now, added, "Me and Sam were watching the show, but Jake and your dad were halfway to the lake, trying to stay out of range."

"Did they get in trouble?" Eric asked.

Donna, grinning in memory, spoke up as she joined them. "Jake and your dad had to clean the whole house, top to bottom. Then they had to help Jeremiah install the new washing machine that was delivered the next day." She walked up to her son, kissed his forehead and took his can of soda for a drink. "The two of them were in charge of laundry duty the rest of that summer."

"Hi, Donna," Sam said, walking up to give her a hug.

"Donna," Cooper told her, giving her a welcome kiss, "you just get prettier all the damn time."

"Uh-huh," she said, smiling at both of the men before turning a wary eye on Jake.

He nodded at her and Donna had to force herself not to go to him. Not an easy task.

Inhaling sharply, deeply, she asked, "So what're you guys up to?"

"Telling tall tales while Eric helps Jake work on that bike of his," Cooper said.

"Just like the old days," Sam mused. "Jake and Mac were always working on something together."

"My dad was good at this stuff, huh?" Eric said, his gaze darting between the three men.

"Damn good," Jake said. "Smart, too. He was all set to go to MIT…" His voice trailed off and the three Lonergan men all shared a moment of re-membered pain.

"He was very smart, honey," Donna said into the strained silence. "Just like you."

Eric frowned. "Yeah, but I don't want to go to college."

"Yeah, but you're going," Donna said, sliding into a familiar argument.

"Damn right you are," Jake said tightly.

"Gotta go to college, kid," Cooper added.

"Your dad would've wanted you to," Sam pointed out.

Suddenly Eric's features froze up and he glared

at each one of them. "It's up to *me*. If I don't want to go, I don't have to."

"Eric—"

"No, Mom. I told you, I don't have to go. I can do other stuff."

"Not now," Donna said, feeling each of the Lonergans watching her, wondering.

She'd been saving and planning for Eric's college education since he was a baby. She didn't have much, granted, but she planned to get loans. Do whatever she had to. Her son was *going* to college. She hadn't gone—hadn't really been able to. But Eric was going to get every chance she could give him.

Unfortunately Eric was all too aware of how little money there was and he'd determined just last year, that he wasn't going to go to school. This was an ongoing argument and one she had every intention of winning. She also had no intention of bringing the Lonergans into a private battle.

"Jake didn't go to college and *he* turned out okay," Eric argued.

"Don't use me as an example, kid," Jake muttered darkly.

"We are not talking about this now, Eric," Donna said, giving her son the glare that usually quieted him right down and forced him to take a backup step.

"Donna," Sam spoke up abruptly. "Maggie's

cooking up a truckload of fried chicken. You and Eric want to stay for dinner?"

She opened her mouth to say *no,* when Eric turned his big, dark eyes on her in a silent plea. He needed this, she reminded herself. And besides, if all three Lonergans stood beside her on the issue of college, maybe it was a good thing for Eric to spend extra time with them.

But that wasn't the real reason she wanted to stay as badly as Eric did and she knew it. Couldn't say so out loud of course, but there was no point in trying to lie to herself. She wanted to stay because she'd missed Jake over the last few days. And since she couldn't trust herself to be alone with him, staying for dinner with the family was as good as she was going to get.

Stomach sinking, throat tightening, she surrendered to the inevitable. "Sure, Sam, that would be great, thanks. I'll just call my mom and let her know."

Eric gave her a brief, fierce hug, then sprinted for the house. "I'll call Grandma!"

Jake watched Donna standing there shell-shocked and couldn't be sorry she'd been guilted into staying for dinner. Just looking at her was almost enough to ease the ache inside him. Though touching her would be a hell of a lot better.

But first, he had something to say to her. Something he, Sam and Cooper had already talked over. He tore his gaze from Donna and looked from one of his cousins to the other, getting their silent okays before speaking.

"Donna, about Eric's college…"

She stiffened and he could actually *see* her pride kick in. "Eric's schooling is nothing for you guys to worry about. I appreciate you all taking my side in this, helping me to convince him to go to college. But as for his schooling itself, he's my son and I'm taking care of it."

"He's Mac's son, too," Sam said quietly and her gaze snapped to his.

"And we figure we're sort of representing Mac's interests," Cooper added, earning himself a glare from Donna.

"Well," she said, "you figured wrong. I make the decisions concerning my son. Me. Alone. Just like I always have."

Jake walked toward her and he noticed when she took a step back. He didn't like it. "You're not alone anymore," he said softly.

She sighed and scrambled for patience. "I appreciate that you guys want to be close to Eric. And I'm even willing to admit that it's good for him. He *needed* men in his life. Needs to know about his father."

Oh, it had cost her to say that. Jake saw it in her eyes.

"But you don't owe Eric anything more than affection," she said.

"You're wrong," Jake said and dropped his hands onto her shoulders. Tension radiated from her, but he noted that she didn't step out from under his touch. "He's owed what would have been Mac's."

"What do you mean?" Her gaze was locked on him and he felt the cool strength in her gather, prepared for battle. Was there anything more fierce than a mother standing in front of her cub?

Cooper pushed away from the bench and came to stand alongside Jake. Sam took up position on the other side of him until all three Lonergans were lined up as a unit, facing Donna.

"That last summer," Jake said, not taking his gaze from Donna, "Mac and I came up with this…" He paused, shrugged and said, "No need for specifics—"

"Thanks for that," Cooper muttered, "I hate when you get specific about engine parts."

"Quiet," Sam said, then gave Jake a shove to get him talking again.

"We came up with this little gizmo for engines," Jake said as his memory kicked in, reminding him of all the hours he and Mac had spent in this barn. "It improves performance, helps get better gas mileage. Anyway, with help from Jeremiah and our folks, we sold the idea to a major manufacturer and—"

"What he's trying to say is," Sam interrupted, "the royalties on that little whatever—it—is come to some serious money."

"So?" Donna whispered.

"So," Jake said, his hands tightening on her shoulders, gaze boring into hers, "we each get a quarter of the money. We've been donating every year what would have been Mac's share to different charities. Now that we know about Eric, we want *him* to have Mac's share."

Nine

Donna went cold and still inside as she looked from Jake's heated gaze to Sam and then to Cooper. God, she couldn't believe that only five minutes ago, she'd been having nothing but warm fuzzy feelings for these guys. Temper spiked inside her and fury began to bubble and froth in the pit of her stomach. All three men were staring at her, waiting for her reaction.

Well, she wouldn't disappoint them.

"I see," she said through gritted teeth. "Let's just make sure I get this straight. Every year you give Mac's share to some charity or other."

"Right," Jake said, smiling.

"And now *we're* your new charity?"

Jake's smile vanished.

All three of the Lonergan cousins looked as if they'd been hit in the head with a two-by-four. Three sets of dark eyes widened, three mouths dropped open and three expressions shifted to worry.

"I didn't say that," Jake blurted.

"You *did* say that," she countered, stepping out from beneath his touch so the heat of his hands couldn't slide down inside and confuse her further.

God. Her body was practically vibrating with fury. She was embarrassed and angry and—too many things to try to identify at once.

"Damn it, Jake," Sam said, shoving his cousin until he staggered back a step or two.

"I knew you'd screw this up," Cooper accused, stabbing one finger at him in disgust.

"What'd I say?" Jake demanded, ignoring his cousins to stare at Donna. "What the hell did I say wrong?"

"Apparently *everything*," Sam grumbled. Shooting a look at Cooper, he snarled, "I *told* you we shouldn't let him be the one to bring this up."

"You're not helping," Cooper told him.

"I *still* don't know what I said that was so damn wrong," Jake complained, throwing both hands high then letting them fall to his sides.

"Well then, allow me to be the one to explain it to you," Donna snapped, stepping forward to poke her index finger into his chest with every single word. "We are *not* your latest cause, Jake Lonergan. My son and I don't need charity from the Lonergan boys. We get along fine. Always have. Always will."

"I didn't say *you* were a charity," he countered hotly. "All I said was—"

"Trust me," Donna interrupted and fought down the urge to kick him, "you *don't* want to say it again."

"This really isn't going the way we'd planned," Cooper put in.

"You think?" Jake nearly shouted.

"So, Coop and me will just wander on out of here," Sam said, stepping around Jake to grab his other cousin's arm and give it a tug. "Donna, you and Jake can hash this out and we'll just see you inside when the battle's over."

She didn't even glance at the other two men. Didn't acknowledge that Sam had spoken. Her gaze fixed on Jake, she concentrated on seeing past the red haze of fury that had her vision blurred.

"How could you say that, Jake?" Shaking her head, she swallowed hard to get rid of the knot in her throat, then asked, "How could you even *think* I'd go along with that?"

"Damn it, Donna," he argued, "you're deliberately misunderstanding."

"Oh, I think you were very clear."

"Apparently not," he muttered.

She poked at him again, just because she needed

to. "Yes, you were. Now that you know about Eric, you're going to make him your own private charity. Well, no thanks. That's not what my son needs from you guys."

"It's not *charity,* damn it," Jake shouted and reached up to shove both hands along the sides of his head as if trying to keep his brains from spilling out. "It's what's *right.* It's *fair.*"

"Do you think Eric came around to meet you guys because he wanted *money?*" Donna asked, still riding the crest of the fury pumping within. She inhaled sharply as another thought crashed through her brain. "Good God. Do you think that's why *I* let him come here?"

Scraping both hands up and down her own arms, Donna fought to get control of her rampaging thoughts. Her brain was in turmoil and her body was still—damn it all anyway—hungering for Jake's touch. Even as furious as she was, she couldn't ignore the burning ache within.

Which only made the situation far worse.

Jake sucked in a deep gulp of air and let it slowly slide from his lungs. A couple of seconds ticked past and then he was there, in front of her again, reaching for her again and Donna had to scramble to keep a safe distance between them.

"You're overreacting," he said.

"I don't think so."

"Trust me."

She snorted.

"Fine," he huffed. "Then just *listen* to me."

She blew out a breath, fixed her narrowed gaze on him and said, "Go ahead."

Jake shoved both hands into his jeans pockets as if to keep from reaching for her again, then he hitched one hip higher than the other and locked his gaze with hers. "Of course you didn't let Eric come here hoping to get money out of us. Hell, how would you know there was any to get?" He paused and shrugged. "Except for Coop, of course. Mr. Big-Time Writer has buckets of cash."

"Jake…"

"Not the point." He shook his head. "Ever since we found out about Eric, the three of us have been talking. If Mac were alive, he'd be getting a quarter share of the royalties on our invention."

She nodded, ignoring the tiny twinge of pain at the memory of Mac.

"Well, Mac's not here. But his son is."

"Yes, but—"

"You said you'd listen."

"Right."

"It's what Mac would want," Jake said, his voice so quiet, so low, she had to strain to hear him. "He'd want his son to have his share of the money. You know that, right?"

"Yeeessss…" Of course Mac would have

wanted Eric to have his share. But that didn't make it any easier to accept.

"So we want to make Eric a full partner—legally—for Mac's sake."

Her whole body went limp. Like a balloon that had been suddenly deflated. She couldn't very well argue with that kind of logic. And just for an instant, her mind whirled, showing her how much easier her life could be if she simply accepted what the Lonergans wanted to offer her and Eric.

But almost as soon as she entertained the notion, she let it go again.

"I understand," she said finally, her voice empty of the fury she'd felt only moments ago. Lifting her gaze to Jake's she said, "But how can I accept when I've spent the last fourteen years teaching Eric that people should stand on their own two feet?"

He smiled and carefully moved toward her, as if unsure about her temper and his welcome. "I get that," he said, "but he'll still have to stand on his own two feet, Donna. The money just makes a nice cushion if he should happen to fall."

"I don't know…"

"At least," Jake said quickly, "let us put the money into a trust or something for him. It'll be there for college and for anything else he wants later on."

The thought of being able to send Eric to a good college without having to worry about how to pay for it was just too enticing to pass up. And if the money was in a trust for her son, *she* wouldn't be using it. *She* wouldn't be relying on the Lonergans to support herself.

Relief pooled in the pit of her stomach even as she nodded and said, "All right. I'll agree to the college fund—on one condition."

One corner of his mouth quirked. "You're a hard woman, Donna."

"You betcha," she said, then continued. "The money's to be used *only* for college. Whatever's left has to go into a trust that Eric can't touch until he's thirty."

Both eyebrows lifted, but Jake nodded his agreement. "Okay, we'll set it up. But Donna—" He paused, took a breath and said, "Look. I know you're only doing what you think best for him. But you should be careful with Eric."

"What do you mean?"

He pulled his hands free of his pockets and took her shoulders in a firm, gentle grip. "Don't get all fired up again, I'm just offering a little free advice. Take it or not, as you like."

She tried not to notice the heat from his hands pooling into her body. Instead she focused on his eyes. So dark. So deep. She swallowed hard. "Go ahead."

"It's just…after my dad died, my mom tried to shut me up in a closet, make sure I was safe. It backfired on her. I rebelled every chance I got." He shrugged. "Hell, I even joined the Marines right out of high school, just to get out on my own."

"I remember."

"Yeah well, the point is, if Mom hadn't tried to tie me down so tight, I wouldn't have fought so hard to get free." His thumbs moved on her shoulders, stroking, soothing. "It's not something I'd like to see happen to Eric. Or you."

His words, quiet, gentle, rang true inside her and Donna couldn't ignore them. Eric was getting older, pushing at the rules, straining to be his own person. Donna had spent the last fourteen years protecting him. Even though she knew it was natural for him to test his boundaries, it wasn't going to be easy to learn to take a step back.

"I know you mean well, Jake," she said, not wanting him to know just how hard his words had hit her, "but you're not Eric's father."

"I almost was," he reminded her and her body flushed with heat as flames licked at her soul.

"You're never going to let that night go, are you?" she whispered.

"Nope." Sliding one hand from her shoulder to the curve of her breast, he cupped her, stroking his thumb across her hardened nipple until she sucked in a gulp of air and held it. "Although I admit that the night we spent together recently is a much better memory." He paused. "I've missed you the last few days."

"Jake…" Her eyes closed, then flew open as his hand dropped to the hem of her T-shirt and slid up beneath the fabric. When he reached the barrier of her bra, he slipped beneath that, as well, so that he could touch her breast, skin to skin. "Oh," she said on a sigh, "you so shouldn't be doing that."

"No, we should be doing a lot more," he said, dipping his head to take her mouth in a sweet kiss of promise.

"You're not playing fair," she whispered brokenly.

"Damn straight."

She laughed, then gasped as his thumb and fore-finger tweaked and pulled at her nipple. The drawing sensation seemed to shoot all the way to the soles of her feet and back up again, with a slow, burning pit stop at her center. She'd never known want like this. Hadn't even known she *could* feel like this. She leaned into him, licked her lips and sighed as he continued his teasing touch.

"I wasn't going to see you again," she admitted. "Not alone, at least."

"Yeah, I figured that out," Jake told her, kissing her forehead, her closed eyes, the tip of her nose.

"I have to see you again," she said on a sigh.

"I was hoping for that," he said, dropping his head to kiss her mouth, stroke the tip of his tongue across her lips.

She shivered. "This can't be a good idea, Jake."

"We're two adults with no ties, Donna." His

breath dusted across her face and she nearly whimpered with the wanting. "We want each other. Why shouldn't we *have* each other?"

Donna stared up into his eyes and shook her head again. "You make it sound so reasonable."

Jake grinned and winked at her. "Well, we're making progress," he said, still smiling. "A couple days ago, I was just Danger Man. Now I'm reasonable."

She chuckled and bent her head to rest her forehead on his broad chest. "How does everything get so turned around? So confusing? I swear Jake, sometimes I just don't know what to think. Or feel."

"You make it harder than it has to be, Donna," he said. "You always did."

She lifted her head to look at him and saw those deep, dark eyes of his glittering with a heat that warmed her through in an instant. "No, Jake. I just see the consequences of things. You never wanted to look past the moment."

"People change," he said.

Her mother had said that very thing to her not long ago. And she had the same answer now. "No, they really don't."

"Donna…"

Laying her hands on his chest, she felt the steady pounding of his heart beneath her palms and used that rhythm to regain her own sense of balance. "Jake, it doesn't matter. For right now, this moment, nothing else matters. Just the feel of your hand on me. The taste of your mouth. I'll worry about the consequences later."

His hand covered her breast, holding her, kneading her flesh with sure, gentle strokes. "You shake me, Donna. Right down to the ground, you shake me."

"Shut up, Jake," she said softly, going up on her toes to kiss him.

He pulled her close, his hands sliding around to her back, pressing her body to his, aligning their lengths as he took her mouth with a relentless passion that left her breathless. Tongues entwined, breath mingling, they dissolved into each other, the world drifting away.

Until Eric shouted from the house.

"Mom! Grandma says she's going out with Mike and that we should stay and have fun!"

Donna jolted free of Jake's kiss and choked out a laugh as the back door slammed shut behind her son again.

Jake looked down at the woman in his arms, her features flushed, her mouth ripe with need. "Having fun yet?"

"Oh, yeah." The hell with consequences, she thought wildly, eager for another taste of him.

Over the next week, Jake and Donna indulged in a flirtatious dance that kept them both on the edge of madness. But there never seemed to be time for them to be alone. The families kept intruding. Between the Lonergans and Eric and Donna's mom, there was always someone else around. The occasional stolen kiss seemed all the more sweet because of it, though, and Jake spent every spare minute thinking about what he and Donna would do to each other as soon as they got a chance.

Meanwhile, though, he and Eric spent a lot of time together. And the more he saw of him, the more he saw the boy for who he was instead of seeing him solely as a reflection of Mac.

Still, as he came to know the boy better, Jake's sense of guilt, of regret, grew until it nearly choked him. Every moment he spent with the boy ragged on Jake as he realized all that Mac was missing.

Dying at sixteen had cheated Mac of not only living his own life, but also of the chance to watch his son grow into a hell of a kid.

While Eric carefully cleaned Jake's tools before putting them away, Jake tried to tell himself that Mac would want him spending time with the boy. But even that wasn't enough to completely ease away the old, familiar ache he'd lived with for so many years.

"Mom said you were in the Marines."

"What?" Jake blinked himself out of his

thoughts to look at the boy watching him. "Uh, yeah. I was. Six years."

"Did you like it?"

"Yeah, I did." It had given him what he'd needed most at the time. A sense of belonging. A job to do. A place to bury his pain.

"You think I would make a good Marine?"

Jake stared at the boy's wide eyes and the too-long hair laying across his forehead. He looked impossibly young. "Sure you would," he said, then added, "but if you join up after college, you could go in as an officer."

Instantly a shutter dropped over Eric's eyes. "I'm not going to college."

"Your dad would have wanted you to."

"But he's not here, is he?"

"No." Pain lanced through him and once again, Jake was reminded of all he had and all Mac had lost. How long would he pay for that one summer day? How long must he live with the guilt that surrounded every thought of Mac?

Eric finished with the tools, then turned to face Jake. "My dad was smart, right?"

"Yeah."

The boy nodded. "Mom always talks about it. She always tells me that my dad was really smart. Smarter than most people."

"He was," Jake said softly.

"Well I'm *not*," Eric told him, shoving both

hands into his pockets and rocking back and forth on his heels. "I'm not as smart as him and I'm never gonna be, so I don't want to go to college."

Jake watched the kid and saw pain etch itself into his features. It seemed as though Mac had left a stamp on all of them. Even the boy who'd never known him.

"You don't have to be like your dad," Jake said quietly. "If he was here, he'd tell you to be yourself."

"You think so?"

"Yeah, I do."

"Then I don't want to go to college."

Jake sighed. Hell, arguing with a kid was like walking in circles. No beginning, no end. "You might change your mind."

"That's what mom says. But I won't."

"Eric, you've got plenty of time to make that decision."

"You didn't go," the boy said defiantly.

"No, I didn't."

"And you turned out okay."

"Yeah, but it was harder than it should have been. And there's a lot I regret."

"Like what?"

Jake leaned against the workbench, folded his arms across his chest and stalled for time. Hell, he was so not the guy to be talking to a kid about major life choices. Sam ought to be doing this. Or

Cooper. But as he looked into Eric's eyes, he knew there was no escape.

"Like missing out on the chance to be a kid. To go to school with other kids." Jake shrugged and said, "No point in learning life the hard way, Eric. College is something everybody needs these days."

"You guys gave Mom the money for me to go to college, didn't you?"

It was an accusation, not a question.

"It was the money that would have been Mac's. Now it's yours."

"I don't want it." Eric straightened up and lifted his chin defiantly. "I didn't want to go before and when we couldn't afford it, maybe Mom would have given up."

Jake snorted. "Don't believe that for a minute. Your mom doesn't have a lot of 'give up' in her."

"I'm not my dad. He *liked* school. And I'm not as smart as him."

"You don't know that."

The kid swallowed hard and his Adam's apple bobbed like a cork on a fishing line. "Yeah, I do. And I don't want to go to college just to flunk out."

"Are you flunking in high school?" Jake asked quietly, keeping his voice even in an attempt to calm the kid down a little.

"No, but—"

"So what makes you think you'd flunk out of college?"

He scowled. "I just don't want you guys deciding what I do with my life."

Jake pushed off the bench and took a step toward the boy. "We're not trying to do that," he said. "We're only trying to give you the opportunity to make choices for yourself. To do what Mac would have wanted."

"My father's *dead*." Eric pushed his hair out of his eyes and Jake noticed the sheen of tears glinting in them. "I'm not him."

"Aw, hell, Eric." Jake blew out a breath and took a step closer. "Nobody thinks that. We just want—"

"I'm not smart like him," Eric said. "I can't be him. I can't be what you guys want me to be."

Before Jake could say anything else, Eric ran past him, grabbed his ten-speed and raced down the driveway and out onto the road.

"Perfect," he muttered thickly as he stood alone in the barn. He was doing a hell of a job here in Coleville. Not only had he started up an affair with Mac's old girlfriend, but he'd found a way to alienate Mac's son.

He slapped one hand to his chest and rubbed it as if he could actually physically massage away the pain that seemed to always be with him.

It probably would have been better for everyone involved, he thought, if he'd just never come back home at all.

Ten

When Jake's motorcycle pulled up in front of her house, the deep, throaty rumble of the engine did some amazing things to Donna's body.

She felt the quickening of her pulse. Her heartbeat skittered and her breath shortened in anticipation. Pulling back the edge of the white lace curtains, she stared out the window at him as he swung one long leg over the back of the bike, pulled off his helmet and set it down on the black leather seat. He took off the sunglasses he wore even at night, hooked them in the pocket of his black T-shirt, and started for the house.

"Oh, boy." Donna swallowed hard and told

herself to get a grip. He wasn't here on a date. He'd only come because she'd called him after Eric came home. Her son had been upset and hadn't wanted to talk to her about whatever it was that was bothering him.

She'd called Jake as soon as Eric left to spend another night at his friend Jason's house. Irritating to admit that she needed help figuring out what was wrong with Eric, but if anyone would know, it would be the man who'd spent most of the day with him. And it hadn't taken Jake more than fifteen minutes to get here. His long legs made short work of the flower-lined walkway and in just a few seconds, he was ringing the doorbell.

Opening the door, she stood there for a long minute, just looking at him. Probably not a good idea to have him here when she was alone. Her mom was out on another date with her boyfriend and with Eric gone, too…there'd be no one around to put a damper on Donna's already blazing internal fires.

"Do I get to come inside?" he finally asked.

"Sorry. Sorry. Yes, come in, Jake." She opened the screen door and took a deep gulp of air as he walked past her into the living room. His scent crowded her mind, pushing rational thought out what had to be a hole in her head.

Closing the door behind him, she leaned back against it and looked up at him as he turned to face her.

"Where's your mom?"

"On a date."

He grinned. "No kidding? Good for her." He glanced around. "Eric?"

"At Jason's house."

His grin faded as he walked up close. "In that case, I'm glad you called."

He touched her and she felt a shiver of expectation slide down her spine. Valiantly she fought for control. "I didn't call you so we could—" she waved one hand "—you know."

"Okay," he said, rubbing the palm of his hand up and down her arm in long, slow, sensuous strokes. "Then why?"

"I need to know what's upsetting Eric," she blurted, hating that she had to go to someone else— even Jake—to find out what was wrong with her son.

His hand on her arm stopped. "I think the idea of college is scaring him."

"He's only a sophomore in high school."

"Yeah, well, like his mom, I guess he thinks ahead."

She blew out a breath and sighed, letting her head fall back to the door behind her. "I don't want him to be scared. I want him to be excited, knowing he can go to whatever school he wants to now."

"He's afraid of failing," Jake told her.

"Why? He's so smart."

"That's probably our fault," he admitted, pulling

her to him, wrapping his arms around her. "We've all told him how smart Mac was—and now, I think Eric's feeling pressure to be just like his father."

"Oh, man…" Donna slid her arms around his waist and rested her head on his chest. Just hearing the steady beat of his heart soothed her as much as having him hold her excited every cell in her body.

He rubbed her back with his big, strong hands and Donna closed her eyes, relishing the sensation even as she said, "I just want him to be happy."

"And he knows that," Jake assured her, voice dropping to a whisper of sound that seemed to seep right into her bones. "He's just confused and— hell, Donna. He's fourteen years old. That's a rough age for a boy, anyway. He's gonna be okay."

He would, she knew it. Felt it. But that didn't stop her mother's radar from blipping into life the minute she sensed something was wrong.

"Thanks," she said, tipping her head back to look up at him. Her gaze dropped from his eyes, to his mouth and back up again. "I guess I needed to hear that."

"Happy to help." A slow smile curved his mouth and his hands moved down her back to cup her behind in a strong grip. "Anything else I can say…or *do?*"

She really shouldn't.

She knew darn well that making love with Jake again was just adding fuel to an already impossibly huge fire. But with his hands on her body, she simply couldn't send him away. She needed to feel him inside her again. Needed to lose herself, if only for a few hours.

"There might be one or two things," she said, going up on her toes to slant her mouth across his.

One kiss. Two. Three. Then a quick slide of her tongue over his lips. Her insides lit up and hunger roared to life within.

Hands on her behind, he pulled her tightly to him, letting her feel his erection, hard against her abdomen. "I've missed you," he whispered just before his mouth covered hers in a kiss designed to steal what was left of her breath.

Groaning, Donna gave herself up to the conflagration blasting through her system. Every inch of her body was on fire. His big hands rubbed and kneaded her flesh and even through the fabric of her jeans, she felt the hot imprint of each of his fingers.

Her core hummed and tingled.

Her breath shattered in her lungs.

He took her mouth with a fierce determination. His tongue entwined with hers in a dance of need so ripe, so raw, she couldn't think beyond the next caress, the next taste of him.

"Your room," he growled when he pulled his mouth free of hers. *"Now."*

"Now," she agreed and slipped out of his grasp, grabbing hold of one of his hands as she moved, dragging him across the tidy living room to the long hallway beyond. Up the flight of stairs, she turned left on the landing, hearing Jake's hurried footsteps as if they were another heartbeat, urging her to go faster, faster.

Once inside her room, he slammed her bedroom door shut, turned to her and grabbed at the hem of her T-shirt. "You're wearing too many clothes."

"Right." She helped him, fingers fumbling with snaps and zippers.

While she stripped down to her bra and lace panties, Jake kicked off his boots and tore at his own clothes until he was naked and reaching for her.

Her breath strangled in her chest as she watched him approach. His body, so hard, so muscled, so *ready*. She wanted him like she'd never wanted anything in her life before. And a part of her wondered as he picked her up and dropped her onto the mattress, why her need for him only seemed to grow.

Then she stopped thinking and concentrated on *feeling*. Reaching for him, she frowned when he avoided her hands and bent to drop a kiss onto her flat belly. Shivering, Donna sucked in air and whispered his name.

Moonlight fell through the windows of her childhood room, laying slices of silvery light across the bed and the polished hardwood floors. It dazzled across Jake, shining in his eyes, gleaming on his tanned, muscled skin. The rich, sweet scent of night-blooming jasmine perfumed the air.

He glanced up at her as he moved slowly down her body, lips and tongue trailing a line of fire over her skin. At the edge of her panties, he slipped his fingers beneath the elastic band and tugged, pulling them down, down.

Donna hissed in a breath and waited, watching him as he smoothed his fingers over the heart of her. Testing her slick heat, he stroked her as she whimpered and began to move restively on the old quilt covering her bed.

"Shh…" he whispered, the sound rumbling against her skin. "I just want a taste…"

Donna took another breath and held it as he knelt between her legs, scooped his hands beneath her bottom and lifted her high off the mattress. She curled her fingers into the fabric of the quilt beneath her and held on as she watched Jake lower his head to her body.

She couldn't look away. Couldn't tear her gaze from him as he slicked his tongue over an incredibly sensitive bud of flesh. "Jake—"

He smiled and licked her again. His lips, his tongue, even his teeth worked at her heated flesh until she was a writhing mass of raw nerves. She twisted in his grip, but his strong hands held her in place. He tormented her by suckling at her, teased her with a flick of his tongue, breathed against her and coaxed the fires within into an inferno.

Donna's grip on the quilt intensified as she rocked into his mouth, his wonderful, talented mouth. Her body tightened, spiraling into a coil as she sought completion. Higher and higher she climbed, nearing the end, nearing the searing climax that awaited, just out of reach.

Finally he pushed her over the edge and she called his name on a half-muffled scream as wave after wave of sensation poured through her. Her body rocked and tears pooled behind her eyes at the wonder of what was happening and still, the starbursts didn't end.

He wouldn't let them.

When he set her down on the mattress, her body was still a humming mass of near-electrical energy. She couldn't catch her breath and a part of her didn't care. Who needed air when you could have *that?*

Then Jake was levering himself over her, covering her with his solid weight and pressing her into the bed. She loved the feel of his body on top of hers. Loved the slide of their flesh moving together. Loved the dusting of dark, curly hairs on his broad chest and the feel of his strength against her soft body.

Oh, God.

She loved him.

Her eyes widened as he slid his body into hers. She looked up into his dark eyes and knew the simple truth of it all. She'd *always* loved Jake Lonergan.

She'd tried not to.

She'd loved Mac, too, in a different way.

But it was Jake who spoke to her soul.

Jake who made her come alive with a touch.

Jake who made her laugh one minute and enraged her in the next.

"Donna?" he asked, going completely still, his thick, hard length embedded deep inside her. "Are you all right?"

"Yes," she lied smoothly, wrapping her arms around his neck. "Yes, I'm fine."

"Good," he said, smiling. "Because we're not finished yet."

"Make me feel everything, Jake," she whispered, moving one hand to cup his cheek. "Fill me up so full that I can't think."

He frowned at her. "You're sure you're all right?"

Concern etched on his features, his eyes glittered as he tried to see inside her head. To figure out exactly what she was thinking. Donna couldn't risk that. So she buried her thoughts and forced a smile to put him off his guard.

Rocking her hips against him, she watched him hiss in a breath and close his eyes tightly. "Don't I *feel* fine?"

"Better than fine, babe," he murmured, rolling

over onto his back and taking her with him in one smooth, practiced move.

She straddled him, as she had that night in the grove. She felt his length fill her and Donna concentrated solely on that sensation. Solely on the feel of having him inside her. Reaching around behind her back, she unhooked her bra and swung it off, tossing it to the floor.

Jake reached up, covered her breasts with his big, tanned hands and squeezed her nipples. She looked deeply into his eyes as she moved on him, rocking her hips, swiveling, creating a friction that threatened to set them both on fire.

And when he couldn't stand the torment any longer, he dropped one hand to the point where their bodies were joined. Using his fingertip, he stroked her as she moved on him, until her breath came in short, frantic bursts.

Donna leaned over him, taking a kiss, then another as she surrendered to the fire. He touched her again and she hurled herself into the blaze and this time, she took Jake with her. He called her name as together, they dropped off the edge of the world.

By the time Jake turned into the driveway at his grandfather's ranch yard, it was just an hour or two before dawn. Already, the ink-black sky was lightening to a deep purple and he knew he should be exhausted.

He and Donna had spent hours loving each other in more ways than he could count. But instead of being tired, he felt more alive than he ever had before. And that had him worried.

Jake cut the engine so he wouldn't wake the household and climbed off to push the bike into the barn. He stood in the dark, took off his helmet and set it carefully down on the workbench. Mind churning with too many thoughts to single out and identify, he pulled in a long breath and tried to ignore the sense of regret welling within.

"Late date?"

He spun around to face Sam, standing in the open doorway. "What the hell are you doing out here this early?"

Sam strolled into the barn and shrugged. "Jenny Fowler's in labor."

Jake blinked at him. "Little Jenny? Freckles? Braids?"

Sam laughed. "She's twenty-five now. Still has the freckles, though the braids are long gone."

"Man, we're getting old," Jake muttered.

"Which brings me back to my question," Sam said. "What's an old man like you doing crawling back in just before dawn?"

Jake stiffened. "Is that any of your business?"

"No. I'm asking anyway."

"Back off, Sam."

"Relax, Jake. I'm glad for you." Wandering over

to the small fridge Jeremiah kept in his barn, he opened the door and took out a bottle of cold water. Twisting the cap off, he took a long drink, recapped it and shrugged again. "You and Donna look good together."

Yeah, they did. Which didn't make things any easier, to Jake's way of thinking.

"We're not *together.*"

"Is that right?" One dark eyebrow lifted into an arch.

"Not the way you mean." Not the way he'd like them to be.

"Why not?" Sam asked, leaning back against the workbench and settling in for a nice chat.

"Don't you have a baby to deliver?"

He waved one hand. "It's her first. Pains are still fifteen minutes apart. Told her to get to the hospital because her husband's having a nervous breakdown. But I've got plenty of time."

"Great," Jake muttered. Louder, he said, "Well I don't. I'm tired. Going to bed."

"Still running?"

Jake stopped cold, spun around and glared at his cousin. "What's that supposed to mean?"

"You know just what it means, Jake. You ran from what you were feeling for Donna years ago and you're still running."

"Who're you? Dear Abby?"

Sam laughed and idly tossed the water bottle

from his left hand to his right hand and back again. "Not hardly. I just recognize the signs. Took me long enough to see that I was in love with Maggie. Almost lost her. Because I was too stupid and stubborn to admit the truth."

"Which was?"

His smile faded and he set the water bottle down on the workbench. "The truth was, I figured I didn't deserve to be happy. I was so busy feeling guilty over what I let happen to Mac, I didn't see that my own life was flying past."

"It wasn't your fault."

"Or yours." Sam walked toward him and slapped one hand on his shoulder. "Hell, Jake, *you're* the one who wanted to go in after him."

Jake shook his head, old guilt burrowing deeper into his soul. For years, he'd let everyone think that he'd wanted to go in after Mac because he thought his cousin was in trouble. He'd never told anyone the simple, ugly truth. Now, though, he heard himself blurt it out.

"Not because I was worried about him, Sam. I wanted to go in after him because I didn't want Mac breaking my record."

Sam just watched him, keeping quiet, silently offering to listen if he wanted to talk. And finally, after all these long years, Jake felt the words bursting from him, as if they'd been dammed up for way too long.

"I was so jealous of Mac I couldn't see straight," he admitted, the words tasting sour in his mouth. "He had everything. He lived in Coleville year-round. He had both his parents. He had brains. And he had *Donna*."

"Jake—"

"No." He held up one hand to cut his cousin off. "Stupid, but God, I envied him. And then that last day—I thought he was going to break my record. The one thing that was *mine*. I didn't want him to. And while I was standing there worried about my idiotic *record* for holding my breath, Mac was dying."

"We didn't know that. We couldn't have changed it."

"Doesn't seem to matter," Jake ground out tightly, feeling the sharp sting of tears. He squeezed his eyes shut until he was reasonably sure those tears wouldn't fall, then he opened them again and looked at Sam. "Mac's gone. I'm spending time with his son. I'm sleeping with his girlfriend." Shaking his head, he acknowledged the truth that had hit him on his ride home from Donna's house. "I can't do this to Mac, Sam. I've got to leave town. Tonight."

Sam scowled at him. "We gave Jeremiah our word that we'd stay for the summer."

"I know but—"

"Jake," Sam said, "you really think you're the only one of us dealing with what happened that day? The only one of us who feels guilty for living?"

"No, but—"

"Running from what you feel for Donna won't help, Jake. Hell, you've been running for years, and you're still in the same place."

He sighed and scraped one hand against the back of his neck. He felt so damn trapped. His heart told him to grab hold of Donna and never let go. But his mind, his guilt, just wouldn't allow it.

Sam slapped him on the back. "You need to talk to Mac."

"What?"

"You heard me. Cooper and I have both had to deal with the past this summer, Jake. Now, it looks like it's your turn."

"Mac's gone."

"No, he's not," Sam said softly. "He's still here, because none of us could let him go."

Maybe he was right. Hadn't Jake been feeling Mac's presence here at the ranch? Hadn't he spent nearly every minute half expecting to see his young cousin walk into a room? But talking to him? "I don't know that I can."

"I'm going to tell you what Maggie told me." Sam's voice dropped as he patted Jake's shoulder. "You don't need to run from Mac's ghost. Mac loved you, man. He loved all of us. Do you really think he'd want you to be miserable for the rest of your life?"

"No. He wouldn't." Blowing out a breath, Jake

yanked a stool out from beneath the counter and dropped onto it. Bracing his elbows on his knees, he cupped his face in his palms. "What the hell am I supposed to do, Sam?"

"You're supposed to *live,* Jake." Heading for the double doors, he said, "Now, I've got to go deliver a baby. Why don't you go out to the lake and talk to Mac?"

Eleven

"How's Jake?"

Donna's head snapped up and she shot her mother a look. It was way too early in the morning to be having this conversation. But she couldn't think of a way to get out of it.

Her mom had always risen with the dawn—and since Donna hadn't been able to fall asleep after Jake left, she'd followed the scent of coffee to the kitchen. Now, she was thinking that probably hadn't been a good idea.

Stomach jittering, she slapped one hand to her abdomen in a futile attempt to settle it. Boy, just the mention of the man's name set her off and she wondered frantically if her mother could tell simply by looking at her, what she and Jake had been up to last night.

"He's fine, I guess. Why?"

"Oh," Catherine said, humming to herself as she stirred chocolate chips into the batter for cookies, "no reason. Just…wondering."

"Uh-huh." Donna shifted her gaze back to the checkbook she was struggling to balance. Too early in the morning to think, but she had to keep busy. Had to keep from remembering the night and how good Jake had felt. Especially with her mother so close by. The woman had some sort of radar.

Glaring at her checkbook balance, Donna muttered a curse. How hard could this possibly be? She knew how to add and subtract. How could her balance be so wildly different from the bank's? Maybe, though, she was just too tired to think straight.

Shaking her head, she said simply, "Let it go, Mom."

"I'm not going to do that, honey." Carefully she dropped a tablespoonful of dough onto a cookie sheet. "If you think I'm blind to what's going on between you two, you're wrong."

Sighing, Donna leaned back in her chair, kicked her legs out in front of her and crossed her feet at the ankles. Folding her arms over her chest, she cocked her head to watch her mom. "And if you think I'm going to talk to you about it, you're wrong."

After she'd filled the cookie sheet, Catherine carried it to the oven, opened the door and slid it inside. Closing the door again, she set the timer, then turned around to face her daughter. "Honey, you know how important you and Eric are to me, right?"

"Yeesss…" Wondering what was coming on the heels of that statement, Donna prepared herself.

"I want you both to be happy."

"I know that."

"And Eric is so enjoying himself with the Lonergans."

"I know that, too."

"But do you know how much *you're* enjoying yourself?"

"Mom…" Donna straightened up in her chair.

"Honey." Catherine moved quickly, took the chair next to her daughter and sat down. Reaching out, she cupped one of Donna's hands in hers and continued. "You're in love with Jake."

Oh, God. She'd only realized that terrifying fact herself the night before. How had her mother picked up on it? That blasted radar thing again. A flush of heat swept through her and Donna resolutely battled it back.

"Mom," she said, hedging the truth, "I can't be in love with Jake."

"I notice you didn't deny it," her too-astute

mom said, then asked, "For heaven's sake, why can't you?"

"Because he's open roads and I'm picket fences." The simplest answer. The one truth she'd finally accepted about five this morning. Even while her body was still dancing a happy jig, she'd had to face the cold hard facts. No matter how good things seemed between her and Jake, it wasn't going to last. It couldn't.

"It doesn't matter what I feel for him. We're too different. We want different things."

Catherine slapped her daughter's hand.

Surprised, she yelped, "Ow."

"Honestly, Donna," her mother said, frowning at her. *"It doesn't matter what you feel?* That's the only thing that *does* matter."

"How can you say that to me?" Donna asked. "I have Eric to think about. His future to protect."

"Protect from *what,* exactly? Love?"

"Mom…"

"Honey, I know you're scared." Catherine leaned back in her chair. "Heaven knows I was scared myself. So frightened, I almost ignored what I felt for Mike because of the fear. But if you could see yourself the way I've seen you the last couple of weeks…you've come alive since Jake came back to town."

Jumping up from her chair, Donna paced the kitchen's length, turned around and paced her way back again. It seemed she was going to have this talk whether she wanted to or not.

Shaking her head, she talked, more to herself than her mother. "When I see Jake, everything inside me wakes up. Sounds silly," she admitted, then kept talking. "But there it is. I didn't expect this. Didn't *want* this." She flashed her mother a steely look. "I loved Mac, you know? I know I was only fifteen, but I did love him. And he died."

"It was a terrible accident, honey. But you can't live your life by that one tragedy."

"How can I not?" Donna demanded. "Look at Jake. He's an accident waiting to happen! The man races motorcycles, for heaven's sake. He loves living on the edge. He loves risk. Danger. If I let myself love him and then lost him…how could I live through that?"

Catherine stood up, put her hands on Donna's shoulders and looked deeply into her eyes. "Sweetie, if you don't let yourself love him, you've *already* lost him."

An hour later at the lake, Jake stood on the tree-lined ridge and looked down on the still surface of the water. As he watched, a soft wind whispered across the lake and tiny ripples stretched out, racing each other toward shore.

"Talk to Mac." Choking on a half laugh, Jake shook his head and glanced from the lake to the sky and back to the water again. Was Sam right? Was Mac's spirit, or whatever, trapped here because his cousins hadn't let him go? Had he been waiting here for fifteen years for the three of them to come back together? To finally face that long-ago day and put it in the past where it belonged?

He rubbed his eyes briefly, massaging the headache that was pounding through his brain with every beat of his heart. Jake felt like a damn fool, entertaining such ridiculous notions. But at the same time, there was a sense of…closure gathering around him. Even if Mac wasn't here anymore. Even if he'd long ago gone on to whatever was waiting for all of them, Jake realized he'd needed to come to the lake.

To tell his long-dead cousin just what he was feeling. To finally and at last, admit to all the crap he'd been carrying around inside him for years.

"Sam says if I talk to you I'll feel better." Dropping to the sun-warmed grass, Jake rested his arms on his up-drawn knees and sighed. "Doesn't make much sense I guess, but I'm so tired of feeling bad, Mac. Of remembering you and feeling pain." He frowned to himself and whispered, "I don't even know what the hell to say to you. 'I'm sorry' doesn't seem like enough. But what else is there?"

A cool breeze whipped up out of nowhere, drifted past him, swirling around him and then dancing on to rush across the open land surrounding the ranch lake. He smiled and imagined that Mac really was there. He could almost feel his presence. Imagination? Probably. But it was a comforting thing nonetheless.

"Eric's a great kid," he said, voice soft. "You'd be proud of him. But hell, you probably keep an eye on him all the time, don't you?" This talking to Mac wasn't as weird as he'd expected it to be. Felt almost natural. But then, the hard part was just beginning. "And if you're keeping an eye on Eric, I guess you know what's been going on between me and Donna, too."

He frowned, yanked up a handful of dry grass and shredded it between his fingers. "I love her, Mac. More than I ever thought I could love anyone." Just saying the words out loud resonated with Jake on a level he hadn't accepted yet. But it felt so right. So real. He loved Donna.

A jolt of pure, male panic shot through him at the thought and Jake pulled in a long, deep breath. "I don't know what that means—for either of us. Hell, didn't know I loved her until just this minute. Shouldn't surprise me, though, I guess. Even when we were kids, I cared for her. Didn't want you to know, of course. But now, you have to know. I tried to steal her from you one night back then— but she ran from me. Back to you."

He swallowed a knot of bitter awareness and forced himself to say the words he'd felt so desperately back then. "I hated you for that. Hated you for having her. Hated you for having what I wanted so badly."

Tipping his head back, he stared up at the wide sweep of blue sky and the white clouds sailing across its surface. "And I loved you, too," he admitted. "No matter how mad or jealous I was, I loved you." The pain inside eased a little and the relief that coursed through him was so sharp and sweet, it was nearly painful. "God, Mac, I've missed you. We've *all* missed you."

Sunlight glittered against his eyes, blurring his vision and making the world seem a little wavery, a little less distinct. And in a heartbeat, his mind's eye drew up an image of the Lonergan boys as they'd been that long-ago summer. Young and fearless, the four of them had expected to be together forever.

"And in a way," Jake said softly, feeling peace begin to slide into his heart, "we will be together always. You're a part of us, Mac. None of us will ever try to forget that again."

The sigh of the wind carried the memory of long-ago laughter and Jake smiled as the past slipped behind him and the future opened up in front of him.

Two days later, Eric slammed into the kitchen and glared at his mother. "Jake's leaving."

Donna dropped the pan she was holding and the clattering bang of it echoed throughout the room. She hadn't seen him since that last night in her bedroom. Was he packed and leaving? Already? Without a word? "He is?"

"When summer's over," Eric said, stomping his way across the room to the refrigerator. He yanked the door open, grabbed a soda and slammed the door closed again. "Jeremiah says he's going back to Long Beach."

Slowly, calmly, Donna picked up the pan, finished drying it and bent to put it into the proper cabinet. Then he would still be here for another week, she thought, remembering that each of the Lonergans had promised Jeremiah to spend the summer in Coleville.

One week. Just seven short days and Jake would be gone again. How was she supposed to go back to living her life the way it had been before he'd crashed into the center of things? How was she supposed to face a future that didn't have Jake in it?

Misery filled her, but she fisted her hands and forced a smile so her son wouldn't know what was going on in her mind. Hoping her voice sounded calmer than she felt, she said, "You knew Cooper and Jake would be leaving at the end of summer, Eric."

"He doesn't have to go, though," her son argued passionately. His cheeks were red, his hair, hanging down into his eyes, hid the glimmer of tears he was trying desperately not to shed. "You could make him stay."

"What?"

"I know he likes you. He told me. So ask him not to go."

Her heart ached as she looked at the boy she loved so much. He was growing up fast and in no time at all, he'd be gone, moving on into his own life. He was already leaving her behind one tiny step at a time. Even her mother was pulling further away from her. Just the night before, she'd accepted Mike's proposal. Soon she'd be married and moving in with her new husband.

Everyone but Donna was moving forward.

Soon everyone but her would have a life. And she'd end up here. In the house where she'd grown up.

Alone.

She didn't like the sound of that at all. No more laughter in the middle of the night. No more stolen kisses or the sigh of his breath on her neck as she slept. No more arguments followed by amazing kisses. How empty her future suddenly sounded.

Oh, a part of her wanted to do just what Eric asked. She wanted to drive out to the Lonergan ranch right this minute and beg Jake not to leave.

But how could she? How could she risk the pain of loss again? At fifteen, she'd been in love as only a teenager could be, and Mac's death had nearly destroyed her. Now, what she felt for Jake was so much bigger, richer, deeper…if he should die—how would she ever survive it?

No.

Better to be safe than wounded.

Alone than devastated.

"I can't, Eric," she said, taking a step toward him even as he stepped back and away from her. A twinge of new pain erupted inside her as she watched his dark eyes flash with fury and disappointment.

"You mean you won't."

"I don't expect you to understand," she said, keeping her voice low and calm, though inside she felt like screaming. "But I have to do what I think is best for both of us."

"You're wrong."

"Maybe," she admitted, acknowledging the ache that had now spread from her heart to encompass all of her body. "But that's the chance I have to take."

Jake took a deep breath of the cool night air and realized that summer was almost over. And if his life hadn't changed dramatically in the last couple of weeks, he'd be thinking about leaving now. Just the thought of that fisted his stomach. But he eased the tension back by reminding himself that things were different, now.

He hunched deeper into his black leather jacket

in response to a sudden, cold wind, and shoved both hands into the pockets. Walking out across the fields, he turned and looked back at the lamplit windows of the ranch house about a half mile away.

It was late, so the house was quiet, but it stood there in the darkness, looking like a safe harbor in a stormy sea. Which is exactly what that house— this place—had always been for Jake. And God, he'd missed being able to come back to Coleville. Being able to have this place to call home.

Smiling to himself, he started walking again, paying no attention to where he was going. It just felt good to be out under the sky. He'd left the sleeping house behind because he'd needed time alone. Time to think. Time to say goodbye to his old world and hello to what he hoped would be the next chapter in his life.

He'd spent the last two days tying up the loose ends of his past. He'd spent hours on the phone with Realtors and bankers, trying to shut down his business in Long Beach and arrange to have it reopened here, in Coleville. Smiling, he told himself he could build custom bikes anywhere. As to the shelter and everything else he had a hand in, he'd hire a manager to deal with the day-to-day stuff and drive down himself if he was needed.

But from now on, Coleville would be home.

He'd come full circle, and damned if it didn't feel good. Right.

He knew he should be talking to Donna about all of this, but he wanted everything settled first. Wanted to be able to tell her he was leaving his old life behind so he could build a new one. With her. And Eric.

And hope to hell that's what she wanted, too.

"Taking a chance, here, Jake," he muttered. "She might just tell you to get lost. Then what?" Stopping short, he frowned at the realization that Donna might not be interested in having him around full-time. A summer affair was one thing. Day-to-day living was something else. Hell, as much as he wanted it, the thought of all that togetherness even scared *him* a little. What if he screwed it up? What if he let Donna down? Let Eric down? What if he just wasn't cut out for the home-and-hearth gig?

What if none of this mattered and Donna didn't want him? Shaking his head, he scraped one hand across his face, smiled and started walking again. He'd lived most of his life by taking chances—risking his neck for nothing more than a trophy and a check.

This time he was risking more than his neck, though. It was his heart on the line, as well—but the possible payoff was so much greater than anything he'd ever known before. Hell, he hadn't even told his family what he was up to. This was too important. Too big. He had to talk to Donna before he told anyone else what he was up to.

Since that morning at the lake, when he'd finally settled things with Mac, he was looking at the world with clear eyes for the first time in far too long. Every breath was a blessing because it wasn't stained with guilt, regret. Every kiss of the wind held a promise for a future he would never have been able to see before coming home again.

In the distance, he heard the muffled roar of a high-performance engine. Stopping, Jake cocked his head to listen as whoever it was drove off, the rumbling noise slowly fading away. Then he shrugged it off and kept walking. Before Donna, his blood would have quickened and his interest would have piqued at the familiar memory of high speeds and excitement. Not anymore, though.

Grinning, he lengthened his stride across the fallow fields. "Tomorrow, I ask Donna to marry me. And that's enough excitement for *any* man."

Donna paced in the kitchen, clutching the phone to her ear. Listening to the ringing on the other end of the line, she pulled back the kitchen curtains, stared out at the darkness and just managed to squelch a whimper.

Where was Eric?

She hadn't seen him since that afternoon, when they'd had the argument over Jake. She'd wanted to give him a little space. But now as the clock edged toward midnight and there was still no sign of him, worry was turning to sheer panic. Now, she was only praying that her son was safe and sound at Jason's house.

"Hello?" A woman answered, only half-awake.

"Vickie?" Donna spun about, twining her fingers around the curling phone cord to the old wall phone. "I'm so sorry to wake you up. But is Eric there with Jason?"

"What? Donna?" The other woman was clearly trying to wake herself up, but doing a slow job of it. "Eric? No, Eric's not here."

A sinking sensation opened up inside her and Donna felt fear roar into life. "Are you sure?" she managed to ask.

"I'm sure, Donna," her friend said, awake now and starting to pick up on the worried vibe. "Jason's at my mom's house tonight. It's just me and Joe here."

"Oh, God." She pushed her hair back from her face and tried not to shriek. Where could he be? With Jake? Would he have gone all the way out to the Lonergan ranch in the middle of the night? But if he was there, Jake would have called her. Wouldn't he? And if Eric wasn't there, then *where* was he?

"Donna, don't worry," Vickie said, though the tremble in her voice clearly said that *she* would be, in Donna's place. "You know he's okay. What kind of trouble could he find in Coleville?"

"True," Donna said firmly, fighting her demons, determined to *will* her son into safety. "He's fine. He's just lost track of time. You know how kids are..." Eric never lost track of time. Eric never missed his curfew. Eric never made her worry and wonder.

Oh, God, where is he?

Then the line clicked and she said quickly, breathlessly, "I'm being beeped. It's probably him. Bye, Vickie." She tapped the call waiting button and said eagerly, "Eric?"

"Ms. Barrett?" A deep voice. One she didn't recognize.

"Yes."

"This is the highway patrol..."

Still clutching the receiver to her ear, Donna slid down the wall and dropped to the floor.

Twelve

St. Charles Hospital sat halfway between Coleville and San Jose. Mind racing, heart pounding, Jake made the fifteen-minute drive in just under ten minutes. For the first time in his life, speed just didn't feel like enough.

He parked Sam's truck in the lot, raced across the asphalt and burst through the Emergency Room doors, gaze-scanning the faces of the people gathered in the waiting room. The walls were a pale, mint-green, a TV in the corner was keeping up a steady stream of quiet conversation and the air smelled of disinfectant and panic.

God, he hated hospitals.

Donna's mother leaped out of her chair and crossed to him instantly.

"Jake, I'm so glad you came."

"Thanks for calling me," he said quickly, reaching out to give her a hard, fast hug. Then he asked, "Where's Donna? How's Eric?"

"He's all right," Catherine said, as an older man with graying hair and kind eyes walked up behind her to lay one hand on her shoulder. "Or, he will be."

"Thank God." He felt as every ounce of his strength rushed from him in such a flood he almost lacked the ability to stand up. "Donna?"

Catherine glanced at the double doors leading into the inner circles of the hospital. "She's in there. With him. They won't let anyone else in."

"They'll let *me* in." Jake started for the doors himself.

"She doesn't know I called you," Catherine said softly.

He glanced back at her and forced a smile. He wished it had been Donna who'd called him, wanting him there with her. Wished he had been with her earlier, sharing her worry over Eric. Wished…hell, he wished a lot of things. But none of that really mattered. All that counted was that he was here now. And he wasn't going anywhere.

Nodding, he said only, "It's okay. It's good you called."

She smiled and leaned back into the man behind

her as Jake headed for the doors leading back into the treatment area. He slapped one hand on the opening mechanism and ignored a nurse already hustling up to try to stop him. She took one look at his set, steely features and waved him on through.

Good call.

His boot heels clacked against the linoleum floor and his gaze darted to either side of the aisle he walked. Maroon cotton drapes hung from metal rods around the beds and he checked quickly, quietly, for the one face he needed to see. Finally, at the end of the aisle, he spotted Donna, alone, hunched in a lime-green plastic chair.

She looked up as he approached and jumped to her feet, racing toward him. He opened his arms and she pressed herself to him, wrapping her arms around his waist and burrowing her head into his chest. He held her tightly to him, grateful to feel the racing beat of her heart pressed to his.

"Hey, hey," he whispered, rubbing his palms up and down her back, "your mom says he's going to be okay."

She nodded, still not looking up, not pulling away from him, as if needing the connection. Which was okay by Jake, since he felt the same way. His gaze shifted, taking in the hustling emergency area, doctors and nurses scuttling from one bed to the next, machines humming and beeping, and the occasional moan from a patient.

He held Donna tighter, resting his chin on top of her head. Her scent wafted up to him and he drew it deep inside, using her very presence to ease the sharp points of worry and fear that had been stabbing at him since receiving her mother's phone call.

"He's in X-ray," Donna muttered thickly, tears choking her voice. "But the doctor thinks it's just bruised ribs and a broken leg."

He sighed, relief shuddering through him. "That's good news, babe. *Very* good news."

"Thank God, he stole your helmet along with your motorcycle."

A twinge of guilt poked at him. God knew he was used to the feeling, but this time, it was so much worse. If he hadn't left the keys in the bike, Eric never would have been able to sneak it out of the barn. If he hadn't gone for that long walk, he'd have been there when the kid showed up. If he hadn't come home to Coleville at all, none of this would have happened.

"Oh, God, Jake I was so scared."

"I know," he whispered. "Me, too."

Inhaling sharply, deeply, Donna gathered the frayed edges of her ragged emotions and pulled back in the circle of his arms. She'd been sitting here in this terrible place for the last twenty minutes, alone but for the torrents of thoughts racing through her mind.

Hearing from the police that Eric had stolen Jake's motorcycle and then tried to take it out onto the highway had stunned her. He'd never done anything like that before in his life. And just thinking about what *might* have happened—if he hadn't been wearing Jake's helmet…if he'd crashed the bike into someone else…if he'd *died*…

Glaring up at Jake through tear laden eyes, she accused, "He was on your motorcycle."

Jake winced. "Your mom told me. He must have taken it while I was out of the house."

She pulled her arms out from around his waist, clenched one hand into a fist and slammed it into his chest. "If you hadn't let him work on that stupid bike," she muttered thickly. "Told him about all those damn races you enter…" She hit him again and noticed that his expression never changed. Concern shone in his eyes along with something deeper, warmer.

But her fear was in charge now along with the well of relief that things had not been worse. "Damn it, Jake, he's just a kid. He never should have gone anywhere near that bike. Never should have tried to ride it. He could have been—"

She broke off, unable to even voice the hideous thought that kept worming through her brain with a sly greasiness to churn her stomach and tear at her heart.

"He's fourteen, Donna," Jake whispered. "That's

pretty much a stupid age. Boys do dumb things. Risky things. It's all part of growing up."

"Stealing motorcycles and going on joyrides is part of growing up?"

"I didn't say it was right—but I do understand it. And the point is, he's okay, babe," Jake whispered, gathering her in close again, holding her tightly to him, despite the rigid stiffness of her spine.

"No, the point is, I might have lost him tonight."

"But you didn't," he reminded her, a muscle in his jaw ticking spasmodically. "*We* didn't."

"I can't do this, Jake," she whispered, voice breaking as she stared up into his eyes. "If something had happened to him—"

"Donna, he's okay. He's alive. He's safe." He cupped her face with his hands, forcing her to look into his eyes. "I'm here with you. You're not alone. *We're* not alone."

"I have been for so long…"

"I know, babe," he whispered, thumbs easing her tears from beneath her eyes. "And you've done a hell of a job." He took a breath, let it ease out again and said, "I'm sorry. I shouldn't have left the key in the damn bike. If I hadn't…"

Donna saw the pain in his eyes and knew, for the first time in her life, that someone else was feeling exactly what she was. She felt his strength, and drew comfort from it. Read fear in his eyes and knew that he would face that fear and do whatever he had to do to conquer it. Felt the love in his hands and knew she couldn't live without it.

God help her, she'd been alone so long, it felt wonderful to have him here with her. To have him hold her and comfort her, to know that he loved Eric as much as she did. That he shared her fear and her relief.

And just like that, her anger drained away again, leaving her trembling. "I'm sorry, Jake. I'm sorry. It's not your fault, I know that. I'm just—"

"I know, Donna," he whispered, kissing the top of her head, whispering into her hair. "I feel it, too."

"Hold me, okay?" she murmured. "Just don't let me go."

"Not a chance."

Minutes crawled past and they stood, separate and apart from everyone else in the hospital. Together, they waited and when the doctor finally came in, they turned together, to face whatever he had to say.

"Ms. Barrett?"

"Yes." Donna clutched Jake's hand and drew strength from his firm grip.

"Eric's going to be fine." The tired young doctor smiled at her slump of relief. "I want to keep him overnight for observation. Even with the helmet he was wearing, he's got a slight concussion."

"But he's okay," Jake insisted.

"You can take him home tomorrow."

"Thank you," Donna whispered, turning her face into Jake's chest.

"Can we see him?" Jake asked, keeping a one-armed grip around Donna's shoulders.

"Sure." The doctor smiled, checked his clipboard, then said, "See the nurse at the door. She'll take you to him. We're getting his room ready."

Eric looked impossibly young lying in a hospital bed. His dark hair was brushed off his forehead and a white bandage covered his eyebrow over his right eye. His left leg was in a cast up to his thigh and a pale green thermal blanket was draped over him.

Donna pulled away from Jake, leaned over her son and kissed the top of his head. "I was so worried."

"I know. I'm really sorry, Mom." His eyes were glittering with pain and shame. He shifted a look at Jake, standing right behind Donna. "And I'm really sorry about your bike."

Jake moved up to the bedside, reached down and took Eric's hand in his. "The bike doesn't matter. The only important thing is that you're okay. Although, we will be having a long talk about stealing and driving without a license."

"I know," he said, words slurring as whatever medications he'd been given took effect. "I'm really sorry."

The boy's eyes closed and his breathing

settled into a deep, even pattern. Donna glanced at Jake and gave him a half smile. "I don't want to leave him."

"He's in good hands."

"I know but—"

"Come on," he said, taking her hand in his. "I think we could both use some air. We'll come back and see him again once they get him settled."

She nodded, but reached out and stroked Eric's hair one last time before following Jake down the long hall toward an exit that would let them avoid the waiting room. They'd have to see her mother and tell her the news about Eric soon. But for now, he wanted a moment or two alone with her. The cool night air surrounded them as they walked across the parking lot to the edge of a courtyard.

Moonlight coursed down on the square patch of grass and painted dappled patterns on the ground as it shone through the trees. Jake guided Donna toward a stone bench and eased her down. She'd left the house without a jacket, so he shrugged out of his and draped it over her shoulders. She clutched at the edges of the leather jacket and hugged it tightly to her.

Watching her, the woman who had changed everything in his life, he felt…blessed. Tonight, he'd felt closer to losing all that mattered to him than he ever had before. The fear for Eric, the concern for Donna—if he hadn't already made the decision to stay here, with her, tonight would have convinced him to.

He'd never be able to leave Donna. Even if he were on the far side of the world, he would always wonder about her. About Eric. He would lie awake nights asking himself if they were safe. If they needed him. If they missed him.

And he knew, he would never know peace in his life without the two of them with him.

"Jake—"

"Donna—"

They stopped, smiled awkwardly at each other until he nodded and said, "Go on."

She huddled in his jacket, tossed her hair back out of her eyes and said, "I only wanted to say thanks for being here with me tonight." She inhaled sharply. "I really needed someone— No," she said with a shake of her head. "That's not true. I needed *you*."

"I'm glad to hear it," he said, going down on one knee in front of her, so that their gazes were level and he could look directly into her eyes. "Because that's how I feel all the damn time."

"What do you mean?" The words were barely more than a whisper.

"I mean I *love* you, Donna," Jake said, gaze moving over her features, detailing every line and curve of her face. "I think I've always loved you."

She sucked in a gulp of air, blinked rapidly and

said, "If this is because you're feeling guilty about the motorcycle, then—"

"No." He said it quickly, firmly. "I've lived with guilt, I know what that's like. And, I've finally put the guilt aside, too." He reached out and took both of her hands in his. "But I can't imagine being able to live without you and Eric in my life."

"Jake…"

"Just let me say this, okay?" he asked, giving her a half smile. "Then you can decide."

She nodded.

"I want to marry you, Donna."

Her mouth dropped open.

He held her hands tighter, locking their fingers together as if daring the fates themselves to tear them apart. "I want to help you raise Eric. I want to have more children with you and watch them grow." His breath caught as the words fell from him, and he knew he'd never taken a bigger risk in his life. He'd never wanted anything more in his life. Somehow, he had to make her see just how important she was to him. How good they could be together.

When the words came anew, they rushed from him as if he couldn't say enough, quickly enough. "I want to hold you in the middle of the night. I want to be here for your tears. Your laughter. I want to be the one you call when you need help. I want to be the man you love."

Donna reeled with the impact of his words. But

it was more than that. It wasn't just what he was saying, but what he was *feeling*. All written so plainly in his eyes. She felt his love pouring warmth and strength into her and knew that everything would be all right.

How foolish she'd been to tell her mother she couldn't risk loss on the chance of love. Tonight, she'd learned that lesson all too well.

She'd had fourteen years of love with her son and if, God forbid, she *had* lost him tonight—she still would have had those fourteen years. And she wouldn't have missed them for anything in the world. If she'd never had Eric, she wouldn't have known the mind numbing fear she'd survived tonight—but she would have missed the love, too. Safety wasn't nearly a good enough tradeoff for the kind of loneliness required to protect your heart.

Loving was a risk, true. But it was the only risk worth taking.

"Donna," he urged quietly, "say *something*."

She smiled. "What about the whole Danger Man thing? Traveling the world? Racing?"

He shook his head and grinned at her. "From now on, when I travel the world, I want my wife and family with me. As for the Danger Man thing…honey, I'll get all the adrenaline rush I need just living with you."

Her heartbeat jumped and her smile widened.

"What about your shop? Your life down in Long Beach?"

"All arranged," he said, just a little smugly. "I'm moving the business up here. Took care of the final details today."

Her eyebrows lifted. "Sure of yourself, weren't you?"

"Nope," he said softly, "just hopeful."

"I'm feeling pretty hopeful, too." She looked down at their joined hands, then back up into his warm, dark eyes. "I do love you, Jake. So much."

"Is that a yes?"

"Oh, it's a yes," she said, standing up and drawing him up with her. "Yes, I'll marry you. And have children with you. And love you for the rest of my life."

His arms closed around her, holding her as if she were the most precious thing in the world. And when he finally pulled back far enough that he could look down into her eyes, he said, "I love you, Donna Barrett, and I swear, we're going to have a hell of a good life together."

Then he kissed her, to start their future off right.

Epilogue

The last whisper of summer was in the air. A blue sky, crowded with lush, white clouds hovered above and the sun shone down on the tiny cemetery, laying golden streaks across weathered tombstones.

Sam, Cooper and Jake Lonergan stood over a grave, staring at a pale green, granite marker, each of them silently reading the words carved deeply into the stone.

Mac Lonergan
Gone too soon

Pain came, sharp—then slipped slowly away again.

"Can't believe it took us this long to come here," Jake said, shooting a glance at each of his cousins.

Cooper raked one hand through his wind-tossed hair and kept his gaze fixed on the grave in front of him. "Maybe we all needed to be together before we could face him."

Sam reached down and brushed away a fallen leaf from the top of Mac's stone, his fingers lingering a while on the sun-warmed granite. "I don't think it matters to Mac how many years it took to bring us here," he said quietly as he straightened up. "What matters is that we're here *now.*"

"Together." Jake nodded, briefly lifting his gaze from his cousin's grave to the wide sky overhead. After a long moment of silence, he looked again at his cousins and smiled. "Sam's right. Mac would only care that we finally showed up. Finally came to see him. To say goodbye. And," he said firmly, "to promise we'll never stay away so long again."

As a cool wind blew up, the three cousins stood in a half circle around the grave where their past lay beneath a soft blanket of green grass. And in the silence, they each, in their own way, at last let Mac go.

* * * * *

Page-turning drama...

Exotic, glamorous locations...

Intense emotion and passionate seduction...

Sheikhs, princes and billionaire tycoons...

This summer, may we suggest:

THE SHEIKH'S DISOBEDIENT BRIDE
by Jane Porter

On sale June.

AT THE GREEK TYCOON'S BIDDING
by Cathy Williams

On sale July.

THE ITALIAN MILLIONAIRE'S VIRGIN WIFE

On sale August.

With new titles to choose from every month,
discover a world of romance in our books written
by internationally bestselling authors.

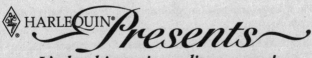

HARLEQUIN® *Presents*

It's the ultimate in quality romance!

Available wherever Harlequin books are sold.

www.eHarlequin.com

HPGEN06

COMING NEXT MONTH

#1735 UNDER DEEPEST COVER—Kara Lennox
The Elliotts
He needed her help, she needed his protection, but posing as
lovers could prove to be risky…and every bit the scandal.

#1736 THE TEXAN'S CONVENIENT MARRIAGE—
Peggy Moreland
A Piece of Texas
A Texan's plans to keep his merger of convenience casual are
ruined when passion enters the marriage bed.

#1737 THE ONE-WEEK WIFE—Patricia Kay
Secret Lives of Society Wives
A fake honeymoon turns into an ardent escapade when the
wedding planner plays the millionaire's wife for a week.

#1738 EXPOSING THE EXECUTIVE'S SECRETS—
Emilie Rose
Trust Fund Affairs
Buying her ex at a charity bachelor auction seemed the perfect
way to settle the score, until the sparks start flying again.

#1739 THE MILLIONAIRE'S PREGNANT MISTRESS—
Michelle Celmer
Rich and Reclusive
A stolen night of passion. An unplanned pregnancy. Was a forced
marriage next?

#1740 TO CLAIM HIS OWN—Mary Lynn Baxter
He'd returned to claim his child—but his son's beautiful guardian
was not giving up without a fight.

SDCNM0606